For my mum: who may not think she's in this book, but she's in every letter of every word, and all the spaces in between.

chapter 1

Why are boys so completely stupid?

My mate Paul and me are chatting as we wait for the bus to school. It's the usual stuff about the latest Xbox game and who's going to win the FA Cup. In other words: normal.

The next minute, he suddenly starts showing off about how many goals he scored at the match we played at the weekend, and how he would have punched some bloke's head in but the referee was watching.

Stupid.

'It was that massive kid from the year above. I would have punched him. I had him in a headlock with my fist ready—'

'What are you talking about?' I ask.

Paul barely stops for breath. 'But of course the ref, who usually never sees anything, had to catch me at it.' He stops suddenly as if it is a natural place for his sentence to end and leans back against the bus stop behind him. 'Oh, hi, Jenny. Didn't see you there.'

It's Goldilocks and her three brain cells, aka Jennifer Gregson, aka Paul's new girlfriend. That explains it. Paul is saying stupid stuff to make himself sound tough. Which he's not. I was at that game and I scored more goals than Paul did, but by the sound of him he was Wayne flipping Rooney playing at his best.

'Hi, Paaaaul,' she drawls, as if she is Marilyn Monroe or something. 'I missed you.'

Paul and Jenny Gregson started going out just before the Easter holidays and then she went away for the whole time. It's the first day back today so really they've only been going out for forty-eight hours. I'm hoping it's one of those phase things that Paul will grow out of.

'Did you get into a fight on Saturday?' she asks.

He shrugs. 'I nearly did. The rest of the team had to hold me back.' He says it as calmly as if announcing he ate breakfast this morning; no big deal.

'That's not what happened,' I correct him. 'He fell into you and you called him a knob, and

2

then he said your Mum was a knob, and that was it. End of story.'

'Oh, heya, Gwendolyn, how's it going?' Jenny Gregson gives me this giant smile that is so fake it almost hurts the air between us. 'Gwynnie,' she says, chirpy as a cartoon character, 'did you do the homework for math?'

'We call it maths in England,' I point out. Jenny went to America. She's obviously trying to remind us all by using American words.

Paul sees Ranjit on the other side of the bus stop and walks over to him. I think he wants to know whether he watched the football last night, which I want to know as well, but I have been roped into talking to Paul's girlfriend. Paul is so selfish sometimes.

I start to tell Jenny my brilliant plan to get out of maths homework. 'I'll just say to Mrs Jakes——'

But Jenny cuts me off. 'Paul is so selfish sometimes!' she says, which I think is really cheeky. Paul is pretty OK as it happens, even for a Chelsea fan. 'You're pals, aren't you, Gwynnie?'

'We're mates, yeah. I've known him for——'

'Well, I'm supposed to be his lady and he fully ignores me when we're out together.'

'I don't know about that.'

'I mean, take a look at him now. Talking to other people while I'm left on my own talking to no one!'

Good to know she values my company.

'Will you speak to him for me?'

'About what?'

She leans in a little and lowers her voice. 'Tell him that when we're together he must have his arm around my shoulders at all times. It shows that he's protective of me. I don't feel like he's being overprotective or possessive enough.' She starts counting off a list on her fingers: the boyfriend commandments. 'If I'm wearing my Jimmy Choos,' (Her Jimmy *Who*'s?) 'they make me a teensy bit taller than him, so he can put his arm around my waist then.' Am I supposed to be taking notes? 'When we are walking it's uncomfortable to have someone's arm around me, so he'll need to hold my hand. Or take my arm like an old-fashioned gentleman. Will you tell him all that, please?'

'Erm.'

'It's really awesome for me to have a boyfriend with a female friend that I have *absolutely* no worries about him ever falling for.' I'm not sure if I like what she's getting at there. 'Thanks, Gwynnie, you're a doll.'

'Maybe you should speak to him yourse—'

Jenny looks panic-stricken. 'He's coming over. Don't say anything.'

'I couldn't if I wanted to.'

Paul comes over with Ranjit. I ask Ranjit about the match.

But just as we're talking about something interesting, some friends of Jenny's – Kimba O, Melissa Rix, Tanya Dawson and Elizabeth Phillips – come rushing over. 'Ohmygodohmygod!' they screech. 'Did you hear the latest?' I can't tell which of them is speaking. It's a blur of red lipstick and gold hoop earrings. 'There's a new boy starting Year 10 today . . .'

'He's starting late because his dad's like some important diplomat or something.'

Me and Paul and Ranjit look at each other like, *So what?*

'So what?' I say.

They direct their answer to Jenny, who hates to be the last to know anything. 'His name is Charlie Notts and he is *fully* gorgeous!'

'I bet he isn't,' says Jenny, who seems a little bit narked. 'Have any of you even seen him?'

'No,' says Kimba. 'But Francesca Ramsgate has, and she says he's H.O.T.' Kimba casts a mean eye over to Paul, who was only vaguely listening up until this point and has now wandered off again with Ranj. 'I'm going to get the new hot guy to be my boyfriend and you can't have him.'

Jenny looks upset, and weirdly I find myself sticking up for her because I'm sort of sticking up for Paul. 'Jenny already has a boyfriend anyway. What does she care about this Charlie Notts bloke?'

Kimba laughs at me like I'm a Year 8. 'Oh, Gwynnie, you are *so* naive! This new guy is in Year 10. He's going to be *so* mature! Not like that Year 9 imbecile.' We look over at Paul and Ranjit. Paul is trying to step on Ranjit's undone shoelace while Ranjit pulls his foot away. He does look like a bit of an imbecile as it happens.

Jenny is seething. 'What does Francesca Ramsgate know anyway?'

Turns out that Francesca Ramsgate knows everything. About two seconds later the hottest Year 10 anyone has ever seen walks over. All the girls go silent and stare at him. Even I go a little girlie. He's tall, with longish blondish hair that flops over his eyes. If we lived in Victorian times I'm sure I would have swooned right now. Instead I turn red. I look at the other girls and fortunately they have turned red too. Charlie Notts has created a blushing epidemic.

Suddenly Paul succeeds in his mission and lands on Ranjit's shoelace just as Ranj is pulling his foot back. Ranjit falls on his bum.

Everyone turns to look at Paul while he raises his arms in the air and does a rubbish sort of victory dance. He repeats, 'Paul is the king and you know it!' over and over again while circling his bum round and round in a properly foolish way.

This makes me laugh and I let out a snort like a pig. I have Charlie Notts's attention. He looks at me like I'm a complete lunatic. I go from Red Alert to Def Con 4. This is the first crush I have ever had and he's already heard my brilliant impression of a wild boar.

'Why don't you go and celebrate with your immature boyfriend, Jenny?' whispers Kimba, loudly enough so that everyone can hear.

Jenny looks angry and turns to me. 'Tell Paul that I'm walking to school. If he can't pay me any attention then I might as well be on my own.'

She storms off. Paul sees her leave and shouts,

'Wait, Jenny! You're the lucky girl who gets to walk with the king!'

Kimba's right. Paul is completely immature. I bet you wouldn't catch Charlie Notts saying stupid things like that to his girlfriend.

Suddenly Charlie Notts looks at me. He smiles. I'm probably just mental, he's probably got something in his eye, because I think he just winked at me.

Big. Fat. Swoon!

chapter 2

Me, Paul and Jenny ended up walking to school – with Paul pulling silly faces at Jenny to make her laugh so she wouldn't be angry with him any more. Most people say sorry with flowers, Paul says it with gurning.

We get to Northampton Hill High at about ten to nine. Late, in other words. 'We'd better go straight to assembly,' I say. 'We don't want to incur the wrath of the Dazzler.'

We call our headmaster – Mr Roberts – *The Dazzler* or *Bobby Dazzler* because of his insanely white teeth. He tells these rubbish jokes and then laughs at them as if they were the funniest thing in the world. Which they aren't. I've heard funnier jokes at funerals.

We have to walk into assembly with everyone watching. The Dazzler stops in the middle of his sermon so that we know that he knows we're late.

'Glad you could join us,' he says. 'Late on the first day back – impressive. Did you forget what time school starts, or just forget your watches?' He laughs, but he's the only one laughing.

I go the colour of the Arsenal strip, which I hate, and not just because I hate Arsenal. I look around to see if that new boy is in the hall. This will be the second time he's seen me and the second time I've gone bright red.

But Jenny loves it. 'So sorry we're a teensy bit late, Mr Roberts, sir. Paul and I just lost track of time.' The whole school erupts into wolf whistles and laughter. It's Paul's turn to blush, but Jenny just grins.

As we walk over to sit by the other Year 9s Jenny, very slowly, takes off her jacket as if it's the most natural thing in the world. Everyone in the school, including me, gasps. Jenny Gregson has ginormous breasts! When did that happen? They are massive! You could hardly notice under her jacket, but with this little top on you can't miss them. No one can pull their eyes away.

Not only are we mesmerized by her properly huge boobs, but also she's wearing a crop top that shows her bare stomach and she's had her belly-button pierced. The belly-button ring is a big blue diamond thing. All the girls start whispering to each other, saying how they want one, or they are going to get one, or that they wanted to get one first but their mums wouldn't let them.

This term is going to be Jenny's term, I can tell.

'Children . . .'

So here we are in assembly, the whole school staring at Jennifer Gregson's boobs, when Mr Roberts says, '. . . that reminds me . . .' He seems to have noticed Jenny's huge knockers (how could he miss them?) and her new piercing. 'I am to inform you that the board is thinking of implementing a school uniform, which will—'

Northampton Hill High completely loses it. There are groans, moans, shouting, begging, and I swear I think I even hear someone start to cry. It's one of those very few moments when everyone in school, however much they hate the year above or the year below, or the goths or the saddos or the hip-hop crowd, all feel the same way.

'Settle down, children!' The Dazzler's trying to calm the mental institution to normal levels of craziness. 'There are ways you can prevent a uniform from being introduced; if, perhaps, you all obeyed the dress code we have, i.e. no rips in clothes, no midriffs on display, no low-cut tops, no short skirts, no underwear showing above trousers, no trousers falling below buttocks.' A few people giggle at the word buttocks. 'Jewellery should be kept to a minimum. No large earrings, especially hoops.' That pretty much includes the whole female population of the school, and some of the blokes. 'And definitely no belly-button piercings.' Everyone looks at Jenny Gregson. 'In short, we want the students of Northampton Hill High to look presentable. If they can't do that wearing their own choice of clothes then the board will have to take that choice out of their hands. Do I make myself clear?'

There's a miserable silence that goes round the hall like a stinky fart.

chapter 3

I survived the first day back but today's going to be even worse. I'm hiding in bed. If I close my eyes and wish really hard, the day might already be over.

I open my eyes. No such luck.

So I get up, throw on the nearest T-shirt from a pile next to my football kit and go downstairs. I am thinking of sneaking through the front door without my dad noticing. I get as far as opening it but my brother, the SAS trainee with hearing like a whippet on Red Bull, calls from the kitchen table. 'Gwynnie,' he shouts, 'get your plaits in here!'

I can picture them both now, huddled together like two conspiring spies who think I'm not on to them. But I am, and I'm dreading the attack.

As soon as I push the door just a little they pipe up singing, '♫ *Happy birthday* ♫'

'All right,' I say, trying to flap them away, 'we all know what day it is. No need to make a song and dance about it.'

Dad's ignoring my *leave-me-alone* tone and runs over to give me a hug. 'Happy birthday, luv.'

'Thanks, Dad,' I mumble. How come he's all dressed up? His frizzy ginger hair is all slicked down straight, his sideburns are trimmed, and he's wearing a suit. 'Is all this for my birthday?' I say, pointing to his fancy outfit.

'I always look this smart!' he replies, and we share a giggle. Dad never dresses up. His tie is older than I am.

'Happy birthday, little sis.' Kevin is grinning. 'I know what the second of April means: cake for breakfast.'

Since Mum died of cancer a few years back we've tried to start these new traditions in the family. We do birthdays at breakfast. With cake and everything. The first year, Dad tried to do what Mum did for birthday tea and it turned out so rubbish we had to start something new. It's not that my dad can't bake or anything, he's actually pretty good, but it was all the other stuff – the tablecloth, the homemade placemats, the balloons with my name on that we never worked out how she found. They don't sell many *Happy Birthday, Gwynnie* balloons at Tesco. Dad tried that year; the closest he got was *Happy Bar Mitzvah, Gideon*. We laughed at the time, but all of us felt really sad. It's those little things that mums just know how to do. They're magic.

Anyway, whatever, that's why we started having cake in the morning.

'I made you chocolate. Is that what you wanted?' asks Dad.

'Is there any other flavour?' I reply.

He plonks a slice of cake down in front of me and I tuck in. It's nice. There's cream in the middle. We all smile at each other as we munch away. Dad and Kevin don't talk much in general, but that's all right by me.

Suddenly Dad gets a bit awkward. 'Look, luv, I know you wanted those football boots for your birthday . . . And I know you've been begging me for a mobile phone . . .' I've guessed I'm not going to like the next part of the sentence as he sort of gets all stuttery and looks at his feet. 'I will buy them for you, I promise. It just won't be for a few months or so.'

'That's all right, Dad, it's no big deal.' I say it too quickly so he knows that it *is* a big deal a little bit. I didn't mean to, it's just the way it came out. The thing is that my old football boots got a hole. Dad fixed them, but they got another hole. I've been playing in trainers ever since and feeling like a right idiot about it. But I understand. Dad hasn't got a job, and the boots I want cost over a hundred pounds. You don't have to be Steven Hawking to do that sum.

'Sorry, Gwynnie. I swear I'll make it up—'

'It's really fine, Dad.' I hope I'm sounding convincing. I'd better leave before he catches on to the fact that I'm actually gutted. 'Got to go to school.' I push my chair away and stand up.

Then Kevin gives me this stare that gets me properly narked because he looks at me like I don't know that Dad isn't poor on purpose and he's doing his best. I sit down again.

Kevin says, 'I got you a present, Gwynnie.'

'Thanks.' It's a box. He's even bothered to wrap it. Part of me must not have grown up yet because I'm still a little excited to see what's inside. Maybe he has chipped in with Dad and they really have got me the boots I wanted. I rip off the paper. It's a shoe box. Good start.

I open the lid and the first thing I see is a pencil. Why would Kevin get me a shoe box full of pencils? I stare at all the foreign objects inside. *What is this stuff?*

It's worse than a box full of pencils. It's worse than a box full of killer bees.

'Er, what's this?' I ask. But I know what it is.

'It's make-up, Gwynnie,' says Kevin.

'I know that. But when did you change your name to Max Factor?'

'You're fourteen now. I thought you might like it.'

'I know how old I am, Kevin, but why would you think I want make-up? When have I ever been interested in make-up?'

Now Dad's the one sending me looks.

Kevin goes all sulky. 'I wanted to get you something special so I asked my girlfriend what she wanted when she was your age, and she said make-up and stuff. She even helped me pick it out.' Then he gets defensive. 'My girlfriend said that a girl of fourteen should be wearing a bit of make-up—'

'I don't need advice from your stupid girlfriend!' I shout at him. (Hang on a minute, when did Kevin get a girlfriend?)

'Don't call my girlfriend stupid,' he says.

'I didn't!' Well, I did, but I didn't mean it like that.

'You haven't met her. You don't even know her. So why don't you keep your opinions to yourself?'

'Look at this stuff,' I yell, getting a little defensive too. 'It's all bright reds and dark blues. So unless your girlfriend is training to be a clown—'

'Do you know what, Gwynnie—'

'Hey!' Dad cuts him off before I can find out what. 'Gwynnie, apologize to your brother. He was trying to be nice. There was no need to be rude about his friend.'

'Why should I apologize? He said I was ugly!'

'I didn't!'

He did, didn't he? Well, that's what it sounded like to me.

'Forget it, Dad,' says Kevin, all up on his high horse. 'If she wants to act like a big kid all her life, then let her.' He storms out like a moody girl.

'Kevin!' Dad calls after him, but the only reply is a slamming door.

'*He's* the big kid,' I mutter under my breath.

Dad turns to me and looks a bit cross.

'Gwynnie, one day you will realize . . .' But he never finishes telling me what I'll realize one day. Instead he looks around the kitchen and says, 'Leave all this. I'll tidy it up later. You'd better get off to school.' He turns around and picks up his shiny green mac. 'I'm heading over to Angela's for a cuppa.'

I decide that I am going to clean the whole kitchen from top to bottom and then he'll be the one to feel guilty. Housework on your birthday equals child cruelty. I'll make sure I do a really good job so he feels extra bad about it later.

Then I take another look around the kitchen and decide that even stubbornness doesn't make me want to touch it. I do what's morally right and leave the kitchen how it is.

chapter 4

I am pretty good at football. Actually, to be honest, I am brilliant at football. I've been playing since before I could walk, with my dad, with Kevin, with Paul. If they're not around then I play with a wall.

It's break time on my birthday and I'm running down the wing, shouting at Justin Kark to pass me the ball. But Justin Kark is a glory-boy ball-hog and he never passes. 'Justin, pass it! Over here, you muppet!' Richard Williams, from the same team as Justin and me, tackles the ball off him and that shows Justin Kark.

'Richard! Over here!'

He doesn't pass it. Richard Williams is a glory-boy too.

When we play at school, the standard rules of football like you see on telly don't really apply: it's about twenty-a-side. One side's goal is from the rubbish bin to the netball post, and the other goal is from this little painted line on the floor to a pile of coats and bags. The rule is that the Year 7s, 8s and 9s have to play on this pitch. The Year 10s and 11s play on the other pitch. That pitch is better and has actual goals on it. No one knows when these rules started, whether it was the teachers or the pupils that made them up, and no one knows who enforces them. It's just the way it is.

I've just shoulder-barged a Year 8 out the way and got the ball. Another year older, and I'm even better at football than I was yesterday. I can see that Ranjit is open on the wing so I chip it over to him. I am not a glory-boy (glory-girl). I'm sort of standing for a bit to get my breath back when I see the new boy, Charlie Notts, at the left side of the pitch. He's frowning as he pretends not to look at the two games, one on either side of him.

Behind Charlie Notts I can see Jenny Gregson and her friends following him and whispering to each other like very unsubtle stalkers.

My team's got the ball back. Better pay attention.

Charlie Notts has taken his jacket off and is

still looking at both pitches. I guess he's trying to decide which one to join. Obviously, as a Year 10, he should be on the other pitch. But the Year 10s are knobs and they won't let everyone play. He looks again at our pitch. The safer bet, but the rubbisher conditions.

Justin Kark has the ball again. 'Justin, Justin, over here!' I shout. But Justin is glory-boying as usual.

Charlie Notts catches someone's eye on the Year 10/11 pitch but they give him a dirty look, so Charlie Notts turns away.

'Justin! Pass me the ball!'

I can see the girls whispering really blatantly and then they all start walking towards Charlie Notts, pouting and flicking their hair, trying to get his attention.

'Gwynnie!' But it's too late. It's the first time Justin Kark has ever passed the ball *ever*, and I've missed it because I'm too busy staring at Charlie Notts. The ball hits me in the stomach, which makes snot come flying out of my nose. 'Gwynnie, you knob!' shouts Justin, and the other members of my team say similar things with ruder words.

The ball goes off the side of the pitch, right in

front of Charlie Notts, and down the little slope into the rain gutter. That's one way to get his attention. I wipe my face and try to salvage some dignity as I go to get the ball.

Ignoring the looks from the girls, I throw the ball in and say, 'Hi,' to Charlie Notts as if it's nothing and no big deal. 'I think I'm getting a cold.'

'What?' he says.

'That's why I just sneezed,' I tell him. 'It looked worse than it was. Not that much snot at all really.'

'Oh.' He looks a little disgusted.

'No, really, it was hardly even half a sneeze. And I got most of it off with my sleeve.' I'll quit while I'm miles behind. I can see Melissa and Kimba laughing at me. I'll try one more time. 'Do you want to play?'

Charlie Notts breaks into a massive smile and for a millisecond my legs go all girlie. 'Yeah. Thanks.' It's the best birthday present a girl could get.

'Cool.' Behind him, the other girls look really jealous. So I act more relaxed. Nonchalant, even. Like I chat to blokes every day. 'You're new here, aren't you?' I say, sounding as calm as a dead person.

'Yeah.'

But I'm not calm. I'm talking to a fit boy and just being next to him is making me want to do the kissing bits I've seen in films.

'Oh, right, thought so.' Cool as a cadaver. 'What's your name then?' I can't let him know that I already know his name and what his dad does for a living.

'Charlie,' he says.

'Oh, right, cool, whatever. I'm Gwynnie.' He nods. I don't think he already knew my name. No one ever knows the names of people in the year below. 'You can be on my team. We're winning. I think it's about 15–10 or something.' I shout over to Paul. 'Paul! What's the score?'

'I dunno!' he shouts back. 'Like 12–7 to them, I think.'

No one ever knows the score in these things. It's not really the point.

'Paul's on our team.' I start pointing the players out. 'Um, there's also Justin Kark, the one that's hogging the ball, Richard Williams—'

'OK. Cool.' Charlie Notts is off and running into the action.

I kind of stand there for a bit and watch him play. Charlie tackles someone from the year below me (I don't know his name). He dribbles down the pitch for a bit. Thomas Ford calls out that he's free. Charlie looks up, sees where Thomas is, and kicks it over to him. The ball bends and lands directly at Thomas's feet with the precision of Gazza and David Beckham rolled into one. Charlie Notts is a footballing god.

'Nice pass, mate,' says Thomas as he jogs up to Charlie and slaps his hand.

Charlie smiles at him and then looks over and smiles at me.

Talk about a birthday treat!

chapter 5

There is no one around when I get home after school. It's a bit depressing to be alone on your birthday with no one there to give a flan. I head up to my room and dump my stuff on the floor.

Fourteen. The big one-four. I thought it would feel different.

♫ *Happy birthday to me* ♫

My bedroom is the little box room next to the toilet. There's just space for a single bed and a small chest of drawers. If I want to hang anything I have to put it in the coat cupboard downstairs, so it's lucky that I only have one thing that I need to hang. It's a dress. I never wear it. Mum gave it to me before she died. But I don't want to think about that now.

My room is papered white with multicoloured dots, and there are some places where I got bored and started pulling off the wallpaper to see what was underneath. There was nothing. In hindsight I probably should have left it.

I suppose I could cover the rips with posters, but I'm not a girlie girl who has a load of pictures of pop stars and sexy actors all over her walls. I only have one poster, and it's of Gazza after he scored from that free kick in the 1991 FA Cup semifinal. Best goal ever.

I plonk myself down on the bed and stare at my reflection in my little mirror. OK, time for self-assessment: My hair is very long, which I think is a good thing. But it gets badly tangled if it's loose so I keep it in plaits all the time. It's somewhere between the colour of bathwater after I've been playing football and the brown of the night sky when it's all light polluted. Even ginger hair like my dad's would be better.

My face is just a face. I've got eyes, a nose and a mouth, so that's a good start, but that's all it is, a start. I haven't got the other thing, that prettiness thing that makes a person good-looking. I will never look gorgeous.

I look down my top at my boobs. They're more like M&Ms that have been glued on under my skin. Not even a half-eaten miniature doughnut hole to speak of. *And* one of them is definitely bigger than the other — more like a coat button than an M&M.

♫ *Happy birthday to me* ♫

Kevin's present catches my eye. I open the shoe box again and tip it all out on to my bed.

There's this blue stuff that I know is eyeshadow. I put some on my finger and rub it on my eyelid. It looks properly stupid, so I put on more.

It looks worse.

There's a black pencil in there and I'm not sure what I'm supposed to do with it. I've heard of lipliner, so I try to trace the outside of my lips with the pencil. It's no good; I haven't got a steady hand so it goes everywhere and makes me looks like one of the goths in Year 11. I don't know exactly what I am, but I know for sure that I'm not a goth . . . I think.

I get out a circular brush thing that's covered in black stuff and kind of poke myself in the eye for a bit. It hurts. I'd better stop.

I look in the mirror again. I'm still skinny. I've still got no boobs and bathwater hair. My face is still just a face. But now I look like I've been in a fight with a load of football hooligans. I'm black and blue, and crying from being poked in the eye.

♫ *Happy birthday to Gwynnie* ♫

There's a knock at the front door.

Oh God! Who's that?

'Who is it?' I shout, while frantically rubbing off the make-up.

'It's me!'

It's Paul. If he sees me like this he will rip it out of me for weeks. I spit on my hands and rub even harder. My whole face goes pink and a bit painful. I think I've given myself friction burns.

'I'm coming!' I shout. I run to the bathroom and try to wash it off, but it's no good. This stuff is permanent enough to stay on but removable enough to smear all over the bathroom towel.

'Gwynnie! What are you doing, you muppet?'

'I'M. COM. ING!'

There is now a blackish bluish pinkish blur where my face used to be, but it will have to do. I leg it downstairs and open the door to Paul. He stands there looking at me with a frown.

'What took you so long?'

'It's nothing.'

'What's going on with your face?'

'I was upstairs.' I realize that I've answered the wrong question with the wrong answer.

Paul stares at me while turning to the side

and raising an eyebrow. 'You know that you're properly mental, don't you, Gwynnie?'

He's got me there.

'Anyway, happy birthday, nutbag. Your dad is over talking to my mum so I brought round the Xbox and I thought we'd give your birthday present a go.'

The make-up is the only present I've had today and I don't see how we can use that on the Xbox, unless we are going to try and make it look ten years younger . . . a Sega Mega Drive.

He pulls out a game box from his backpack. 'Now I know you don't have an Xbox, so we'll have to keep it round mine, but this is a present for you.' He hasn't bothered to wrap it, but it's still in its cellophane, so that's sort of the same thing and that makes it a present. It's the new *Gears of War* game that we've both been wanting to play for ages. 'And I promise I won't play it much if you're not there because it's your game. Until you get an Xbox, that is – then it's properly yours.'

'Cheers, mate.' Paul's the best sometimes.

'No problem.' He pushes past me and walks into the living room to set up the console in

there. 'Oh, and my mum said happy birthday and gave us this.' He pulls out a frozen
pizza.

'Nice one. I'll stick it in the oven.' Angela's
the best too.

When I come back from the kitchen Paul's
already playing the game. He's trying to get his
head around the new flamethrower weapon and
he's failing badly. He's not dead yet though and
he pauses it and asks if I'd like a go.

'But you're not dead yet.' This has never
happened before. 'What are you up to?'

'It's your birthday. I'm just being nice.'

'Fair enough,' I say, and grab the controller.
I'm not missing an opportunity like this.

He stays silent for eleven minutes until the
oven buzzer goes off. I pause the game, but he says,
'Don't worry, I'll get it.'

Now I'm really suspicious. He brings in the
pizza and offers me a slice, but I'm still playing
so I refuse.

His voice sounds all funny when he says,
'Gwynnie, you know Jenny, don't you?'

I'm hardly listening when I say, 'I'm familiar
with her work.' I've just grenaded some locusts
and I'm doing well.

'Well, um, we've been going out for three weeks today.'

'Wasn't she in America for two weeks? Whoa!' I was almost killed there.

'Yeah, but we texted.' He's putting me off so I try to ignore him. 'Thing is —' his voice is sounding really weird — 'she wanted me to get her an anniversary present.'

'After three weeks!'

'And I wanted the opinion of a girl to see if she'll like it.' Paul reaches into his pocket and pulls out a box. 'I don't really speak to any girls so I thought I'd show you.'

I'm intrigued now, so I pause the game, using pizza as an excuse to stop. He opens the box and inside is a silver bracelet with a blue diamond thing in it. 'It goes with her belly-button ring,' he says. 'What do you think?'

I'm thinking lots of things, like: how can Paul like a quarterwit like Jenny? I've heard that love is blind but it can't be deaf as well. I just shrug. 'It's all right.'

He looks really worried.

'It's nice,' I say.

He smiles. 'Cool! Thanks, Gwynnie.' Then he puts it back in the box and back in his pocket.

He stands up quickly and walks towards the door.

I unpause it and carry on playing, but shout out to him. 'I think we're out of toilet paper!'

'No, that's not . . . Oh, sorry, Gwynnie, but I've got to go to Jenny's house.'

'What? You're ditching me on my birthday?'

Paul cringes like he's in an impossible situation, like he *is* actually out of toilet paper. 'It's our anniversary today,' he says with a shrug.

He opens the door but turns back to me before he goes. 'Tell you what: you can borrow the Xbox for the week to make up for it.'

'But . . .'

He's already in the hallway as he shouts back, 'See ya!'

And then a great big locust kills me and I'm out of lives.

♫ *Happy birthday to me* ♫

chapter 6

Why are girls so completely stupid?

I've walked into the toilets at school and there's a group of them, Jenny Gregson and her followers, and they all look the same. Their hair is long and loose and either as straight as French fries, or as curly as curly fries. Every single one of them is wearing gold hoop earrings except for Tanya Dawson, who everyone knows has a mum that is really strict and won't let her do anything. But there is something else that makes them all the same – they are all wearing crop tops, except for Elizabeth Phillips, who is chubby and wouldn't suit a crop top. I guess they think it's OK to look like a fool if everyone else is doing it.

Their heads turn as I walk in. They see me and turn back, as if I am not important enough to worry about. The movement makes something catch in the light and I finally notice what is so weird about them. They have their belly-buttons pierced! When did this happen? 'What's going on?' I ask.

Kimba says, 'Nothing to do with you, Gwynnie,' and turns her back to me.

'Yeah, Gwynnie,' says Tanya Dawson. 'You're not initiated in the BB Club so you can M.Y.O.B. – Mind Your Own Business.'

'What the hell is the BB Club?' I say, clearly not M-ing my own B.

'The BB Club is zip to do with you, is what it is,' says Kimba, thinking she's clever. Apparently being in the BB Club means you pick up Jenny's American-speak like an infestation of head lice.

Jenny Gregson looks a little shifty. This is a tricky situation for her because when me and her are with Paul she's my friend because Paul is my best friend, but when Paul isn't around she doesn't really need to talk to me. She sticks to looking at the floor and I can't really blame her. I'm not bothered enough to care anyway.

'Fair enough.' I make a move to go into a cubicle, but Tanya Dawson is too eager to tell me to let me go.

'BB stands for Belly Button. We're the Belly

Button Club. You have to have your belly-button pierced to be in it, innit?'

'Tanya!' Kimba's angry because Tanya has let out the Big Secret.

'OK,' I say, still not bothered. 'Like I said, *fair enough*.' I get to the toilet door, but then I get confused and turn back. 'Hang on a second. If you *have to* have your belly-button pierced to join, then how come you're a member, Tanya? You don't have your belly-button pierced.'

Tanya tries to think of an answer. 'Errr . . .' I have just picked holes in the entry requirements of their exclusive club.

Melissa Rix pipes up. Melissa Rix is actually in Year 10, but no one in Year 10 will talk to her because she is a bit of a saddo. Our year will talk to her though because she is in Year 10. 'Don't be stupid, Gwynnie,' she says. 'Everyone knows her mum's really strict and won't let her do anything.'

Tanya doesn't look embarrassed when Melissa says this. It's common knowledge.

'Well, what about you, Elizabeth? Do you have your belly-button pierced under your top?'

Elizabeth Phillips goes all red and I feel bad about asking her. 'I *will* get mine done, but not until I lose a few pounds. Otherwise the hole might get all warped out of shape when I eventually shed the weight.'

She looks at the others to see if that's the right answer and they nod in agreement. It's clearly been brought to the table before and they've made their ruling.

'It's just a teensy bit of puppy fat, Elizabeth,' says Melissa Rix, like she's some sort of dieting guru. 'You'll lose it in minutes.'

Jenny seconds the findings. 'Yeah, Elizabeth, and it's really not as bad as you think. If you lost, like, half a stone, you would probably look OK.'

Elizabeth smiles, but she doesn't look happy.

'So, out of five members of the Belly Button Club,' I say, 'only three of you actually have your belly-buttons pierced. I'm not in Mensa or anything, but that's barely over fifty per cent. It's not what I call a hard-and-fast rule.'

'It's not about actually having the piercing,' says Jenny. 'It's more about joining a group of like-minded individuals with an appreciation of the same ideal.'

'The ideal of having your belly-button pierced?' I ask.

Jenny looks at me like, *Duh, of course!*

'Why don't you join the club, Gwynnie?'
Kimba says. 'Oh, sorry, your stomach is so skinny
that the needle would go all the way through to
your spine.'

Kimba and Melissa start to snigger; Elizabeth
frowns, opens her mouth like she's about to say
something, but says nothing. I feel a bit awkward.

'Gwynnie hasn't come in here to be verbally
abused by you,' Jenny says. Maybe she's not all
bad. Maybe Paul is making her a better person.

'Yeah,' I say. 'I've just come to use the bog.'

They all grimace and I feel awkward again.

'Thanks for keeping us up to date with your
movements, doll,' says Kimba, daring to crack
another joke at my expense. Even Jenny can't
stop herself laughing at that one.

I get angry with them and start to shout:
'Your Belly-Stupid-Button Club is stupid. Didn't
you hear what Mr Roberts said at the beginning
of term? Because of you we'll all have to start
wearing uniform! Everyone in the whole school
will hate you! And all so that you can put stupid
holes in yourselves.'

Jenny becomes all teacher-like and tries to
calm me down. 'Didn't you need to use the
bathroom, Gwynnie?'

'OK, OK, I'll pee off!' I put my hands up in an *I surrender* gesture and back my way into a cubicle.

'Perhaps you should go too, Elizabeth,' says Jenny behind me. 'We don't want any incidents.' The others giggle.

'Er . . . Um . . . I'm OK, thanks, Jenny,' says Elizabeth.

I sit on the loo and try to pee as fast as I can so that I can I get out as fast as I can — which makes the peeing so much more difficult. I can still hear them gossiping on the other side of the door.

'Do any of you gals know where he lives?' I still don't know who's speaking as they all sound the same, dropping in American words as if they were raised on the prairies.

'I don't know for sure, but he always seems to come from the direction of Mount Street.'

Who are they talking about?

'And Mount Street is where all the fancy houses are. If his parents are diplomats, he will probably live in a fancy house, won't he?'

There are general noises of agreement.

Are they talking about Charlie Notts?

'OK, so if, like, one of us hangs out near

Mount Street — say, the person who lives nearest Mount Street—'

'You are only saying that because you live near Mount Street!'

'Well, I suppose I do. But it doesn't have to be me,' the voice is backtracking. 'It could be whoever. Just hear me out, will you? Me, or, like whoever, and someone else, hang around Mount Street and wait until he comes by. And we pretend that I, or whoever, have fallen over and twisted my ankle. I'll be good at that because I can pretend to cry real well. Look.'

They make impressed *Ooooo* noises at the pretend crying.

'See. Told you. So then, I cry and he'll offer to help. He's got a cell phone so he'll call an ambulance for me. But when I insist that I'll be OK he'll offer to, like, carry me to school in his arms.'

All the girls do swooning noises because of the thought of this bloke carrying them to school . . . to anywhere . . . to bed. I find myself imagining Charlie Notts carrying me and let out a girlie sigh. *Where did that come from?* I cover it up with a gigantic coughing fit.

'Then, while he is carrying me—'

'Or whoever!'

'Yeah, while he is carrying me or whoever to school we can start talking to him. We can ask what he likes to do after school and stuff, what music he's into, what movies he likes—'

'Yeah, and then we can hang out at those places, like we always go there, and maybe he'll start talking to us—'

'I can't imagine Charlie Notts talking to me.' So they *are* talking about Charlie Notts! 'I'm sure my tongue would fully shrivel up in my mouth and my throat would close over and I would fully die right in front of him.'

'I would be so embarrassed if I died in front of him.'

'It's a foolproof plan!'

I come out of the toilet and say, 'What if he gets a lift to school?' They all look at each other, a little bit panicked. 'Or what if he walks a different way? Your plan is not foolproof . . . it's foolish.'

They all look disappointed. Kimba looks angry and disappointed. She says, 'Come on then, if you're so clever, you think of a plan to get him to talk to us.'

'Why don't you just talk to *him*?'

They stare at me like I'm crazy. Melissa Rix starts laughing. 'Go up and talk to him? Are you mad?'

Someone please tell me why girls are so completely stupid!

Hang on a minute. Why does Jenny Gregson look like she's been crying?

chapter 7

The bell rings for the end of lunch break. Another match is over and we all head in to school.

'Gwynnie!' shouts Charlie. This is what Juliet must have felt like when Romeo was reciting poetry at her balcony. 'Oi, Gwynnie. Oiiiii!'

I turn around and scrunch up my face at him like I have basically forgotten who he is. 'Hi, Charlie Notts.' He's looking at me like I'm a nutter. 'Er, I mean, hi, Charlie. Good game.'

Out of the corner of my eye I see Paul calling to Jenny. 'Oi! Jenny! Oiiiii!' Jenny pretends not to hear him. She is staring at me talking to Charlie Notts.

'Are you guys going to play again after school?' Charlie asks me.

'Oi, Jenny! Come over here and watch my skills!' Paul's still shouting, and he's putting me off. He starts doing keepy-uppies to impress her.

'Gwynnie?' Charlie tries to get my attention.

'Yes. Hello.'

He raises an eyebrow at me.

'How can I help you?' I sound like I work in McDonalds. I hope he can't tell I'm blushing under my hot, sweaty, puffed-out face.

'Can. I. Play. Foot. Ball. With. You. Later?' He's speaking at me like I'm a dimwit and, to be honest, I can't blame him.

All I can do is stare at him like I'm an Olympic musical-statues champion.

'Oh well, if you don't want me to . . .'

'Oh God, no!' Charlie Notts is walking away and I grab him by the arm. I can't believe I've just touched Charlie Notts. 'Sorry,' I say, 'I'm just being a mentalist. It's school, it does that to me. Makes me crazy.' I pull a face like they've just let me out of an asylum.

He laughs. But not in a mean way like I'm an idiot, in a nice way like he thinks I'm funny. Maybe he's not that clever. Maybe that means I'm in with a chance.

'We definitely play every day after school. Definitely. We'll definitely be playing later.'

44

Paul comes over. 'What is up with Jenny?' he asks me like I'm supposed to know. 'She's totally ignoring me.'

I shrug. 'No idea. Maybe the earrings block sounds made by people with an IQ over 35.'

Paul shrugs back. 'That should make me fine then. She's always telling me I'm thicker than a frozen milkshake.'

'Who's that?' Charlie asks about Jenny. 'Your older sister?'

'No. My girlfriend. Jennifer Gregson.' Paul is being a bit funny with Charlie Notts.

Charlie picks up on it and sticks out his hand. 'Sorry, mate. My name's Charlie and I'm new here.'

Charlie and Paul shake hands. 'No worries.' And Paul is over it. That's what's wicked about Paul, he never holds a grudge.

'Heya, Paul. Heya, Gwynnie. How's it going?'

Jenny Gregson has reappeared from nowhere. Everyone's walking inside, and the way they're penning the four of us in makes us into some sort of group: Paul and Jenny, and me and Charlie Notts. Wow, I'm in *a group*.

Then these kids from the year below block my path so I get forced out of the group. Some people are so rude! Already I've been ostracized, after only three seconds of being in a new group. I have to shove the kids out of the way to stick with the others.

Paul goes to put his arm around Jenny, just like he's been instructed to, but she sort of subtly moves away so that he's left hooking the air like a muppet. 'Did you miss me?' he asks her.

'Like a runner in my pantyhose.' Paul and I are not really sure what that means, but Charlie laughs so I laugh. Paul laughs too.

'Gwynnie,' she says, 'I really need to speak to you.'

Why does Jenny need to speak to *me*?

'I'm listening.'

'Me and my gals were thinking of talking to little ol' Mr Roberts. We want to arrange a school prom at the end of the year. Would you like to come if we did?'

'Me?' I ask.

'Well, yeah, you. And I guess, all of you.' She looks from me to Paul and then to Charlie.

'I'll come,' says Paul. 'Might be a laugh.'

'Yeah, why not. I'll go to the prom,' I say. If everyone's going . . .'

'It's not *the prom*, it's just *prom*,' she says.

Fair enough.

We step inside the school and Charlie is about to go to his Year 10 classroom when Jenny steps in front of him. 'What about you? I'm so sorry to appear rude – I don't know your name.'

Doesn't know his name, my bottom.

'My name's Charlie,' he says, and looks at Jenny like all the guys do. Except nicer than the other guys because he doesn't look at her massive chest. He asks, 'Are you American?'

I'm glad I'm not drinking something or I would have spat it out right now.

Jenny giggles in this girlie sort of way. 'Aw, ain't you a honey? No, I am not fully American, but I have family across the pond and I have just spent all vacation over there. There's a chance that I might have picked up a teensy bit of an accent.'

For goodness sake!

'I like American accents,' says Charlie.

Jenny smiles and looks at the floor.

'I do too,' Paul gets in quickly. 'I think your accent is nice. I've said that before.'

'When have you said that before?' she asks. Paul's in trouble again.

'Well, I've either said it or I've thought it.'

Paul's a rubbish liar. He changes the subject by turning to Charlie. 'So, you want to play football later?'

Charlie nods.

'What team do you support?'

Please don't say Arsenal. Please don't say Arsenal.

'Well, I know they can be a bit rubbish sometimes, but I'm Spurs till I die.'

I think I might die right here right now.

'Oh, then you and Gwynnie will get on like a house on fire,' says Paul.

Charlie smiles at me, 'You're Spurs too? Nice one, Gwynnie. It's tough, but we're born to it, aren't we? We'll have to stick together.'

Someone must have lent me their hoverboots because I'm like 200 feet in the air.

chapter 8

There are six billion people on the planet. So what are the odds of running into Kevin on the thirty-second journey from my house to Paul's?

'Gwynnie! Wait!' I don't really know what to do because I can't decide if I'm talking to him or not. I suppose he *is* my brother and I have to talk to him sometime.

'Hi, Gwynnie.'

'Hi.'

'How are you?'

'Fine.'

'So it was the semifinal yesterday? Who'd've thought that Spurs would make it this far?'

'Yeah. It's brilliant.' Which it totally is. But this is all very polite and therefore weird. I'm not looking him in the eye so that he knows that I am still angry with him a little bit.

'Look,' he says, 'I'm really sorry that I shouted at you on your birthday.'

I sort of grunt in reply. The grunt means that I am annoyed but I accept his apology. Sometimes grunts speak louder than words.

'It was your birthday and I shouldn't have had a go at you.'

Grunt.

'I suppose it's just that I thought really hard about what to get you and I was disappointed when you didn't like it.'

Grunt.

'It was probably stupid of me to buy—'

'That's all right, Kev. Don't worry about it.'

'The thing is Gwyn—'

'It's no big deal.'

'But the thing is, is that you are brilliant the way you are.'

This is getting weirder by the second. 'Honestly, Kev, I'm not bothered.'

'You *are* brilliant the way you are: you don't try and be like other girls, which is great.' He takes a deep breath. 'I'm just saying that if you ever want, like, a boyfriend or anything – not that I think you should get one right now – but if you did want a boyfriend ever, you might have to start being a bit more like a girl than a boy.'

I contemplate jumping in front of a car but there aren't any cars coming. Just my luck.

'Most boys like girls. Not boys. Unless, that is —' he draws in a long breath — 'you don't like boys—'

'Oh my God, Kevin, just because I play football doesn't make me a lesbian!'

At that moment an old granny walking past almost falls off her Zimmer frame.

'I know. I know! I'm just saying that if you were, that would be OK. We would still love you.' I can tell he's regretting this conversation because he can't quite look at me.

I give Kevin another grunt and I excuse myself. 'Look, Kev, Paul and Jennifer Gregson are waiting for me.'

'OK,' he says. Then he stops. 'Who's Jennifer Gregson?'

'Paul's girlfriend.'

'Is she Stephanie Gregson's sister?'

'Yeah.'

'No way.' Kevin looks impressed. 'Tell him congratulations from me,' he says, and walks back towards the house.

Why congratulations? You wouldn't congratulate someone for downloading 80 hours of white noise on to their iPod. You would tell them they were an idiot.

*

Right now I would prefer to be in school, sitting next to Rachel Govens in quadruple maths. And Rachel Govens does Sudoku for fun.

But instead I'm sitting in Paul's living room playing *Gears of War* but Paul's not here. He's officially present, but he is in his own little world, snogging the face of Jenny Gregson. All I can do is turn up the volume loud enough so I can't hear the slurpy noises they're making, but not so loud that I go deaf. They sound like our washing machine when it's on the blink.

I get killed by a locust and start to wonder if things could get any worse.

'Your go,' I say.

Paul and Jenny don't look up.

'Oi, Paul! It's your go on *Gears!*'

He says, 'You can have another go,' and I swear to God that he doesn't even take his tongue out of Jenny's mouth to say it.

'I don't want another go.'

Finally he looks up. There is a thread of saliva

running from his lip to Jenny's and I think I might vomit all over Angela's brand-new Ikea rug. Jenny wipes her face and says, 'I've told Paul that I'm not going to come over any more if I just have to watch you two play the stupid computer.'

'Yeah, Gwynnie,' says Paul. 'You're always saying that I hog the game. Now you can have as many goes as you like.'

He turns back and starts snogging Jenny's face off again. I'm surprised she even has a face left. As I start playing I realize it's no fun killing locusts if no one is watching to see how brilliant you are at it.

Suddenly I have an idea. I kind of prepare myself to sound really calm, but inside, just thinking the words is making me feel nervous. 'Maybe I'll give Charlie Notts a call and see what he's doing. If you two are going to eat each other all afternoon then I might as well have someone to look at – er, I mean – talk to.'

This gets Jenny's attention and she's crawled out from underneath Paul. 'Yeah, Paul, we are being very rude to Gwynnie.' It's amazing how that accent of hers drops when it's just me and Paul. 'Why don't we see what Charlie is doing? Because, you know, three's a crowd!'

'I don't have his number.' Paul doesn't look quite as keen as me or Jenny.

'Oh, no problem, I've got it.' Jenny gets out her mobile. Paul frowns at the fact that his girlfriend has another bloke's number in her phone. And not just any other bloke, a Year 10 bloke.

I reach out my hand for her to pass me the phone but she says, 'I'd better call him. It's a breach of trust to give someone someone else's number. You don't want him to think you're stalking him.'

She presses call and she doesn't seem nervous one bit. Sometimes I wish I was like Jenny Gregson. Oh my God, did I just think that out loud?!

'Heya, Charlie,' and the American-speak is back. 'How's it going?' Then she starts giggling.

'What's so funny?' asks Paul, and Jenny frowns at him like, *Can you please be quiet?* So then Paul looks grumpy at me, and I look at him like, *What have I done?* I am only the one that suggested we get him over; she's the one who called him.

All she does is giggle and say things like, *Oh my God,* and, *I fully know what you are saying,* and, *Shut up!* (she so doesn't want him to shut up). Finally, when she manages to stop laughing, she says to him, 'We're all round at Paul's — me and Paul and stuff — if you wanna come on over. They're just playing some game or something and it's real boring, but if you wanna come it could be cool.'

Me and Paul are waiting like Charlie is the referee and he's deciding whether to allow a goal or not. I want him to come over. Paul doesn't want him to come over, but if he does come over then everyone will know that Paul had a Year 10 round his house, and that's pretty cool.

'Oh, I really can't say.' Then she screeches at us in a hushed voice behind the phone, 'What's this game called?'

'*Gears of War*,' we both say together.

'It's some little ol' game called *Beards of War*.'

He corrects her and she giggles. 'Oh, how silly of me! Of course I mean *Gears of War*.'

'The latest version!' I add, as extra incentive.

'The latest version,' she repeats.

We hear Charlie get excited in a muffled way. Jenny gives him Paul's address. It looks like he's coming over.

Now that Jenny is off the phone, Paul is trying to snog her again, but she's putting on make-up and pushing him away. She's always putting on make-up. It must be on in layers so thick that you could dig for fossils. I hate to admit it, but it looks good. She has long eyelashes and shiny lips all the time. I wish I knew how to do it.

Basically, Kevin is right. If I want Charlie Notts to try and snog me the way that Paul is trying to snog Jenny, then I am going to have to make myself be more like a girl.

So here I am, staring at Jenny Gregson when suddenly she catches me staring. I quickly turn away. She acts all angry when she says, 'Why are you staring at me? That's so gross and pervy!'

Paul looks at me like I'm gross and pervy too. I go red and sort of stutter, which makes me look pervier. 'N-no, I wasn't. I, er, just wanted to ask you something.'

'What?' says Paul, thinking that I wanted to ask him something as I never want to ask Jenny something.

'No, I meant Jenny.'

They both look as shocked as if I just said that I wanted to ask the Dazzler for extra homework. I wish that there was a way of saying this like it wasn't a big deal, but there isn't. I'm just going to have to say it.

'Can I borrow some of your make-up?'

chapter 9

Paul's mouth drops open so wide that you could fit a Double Whopper in it. Jenny eyes me like she thinks I'm taking the mick out of her, but once she realizes I'm not, she goes all flustery and doesn't quite know what to say. Which is a first.

'What the hell do you want make-up for?' asks Paul. 'You don't wear make-up.'

'I sometimes wear make-up. You don't know – I'm not with you absolutely every second of absolutely every day.' I am with him most seconds of most days. 'Anyway, you two are being so boring that it's even made *Gears of War* boring, so I thought I'd try something new.'

Jenny stares at me with one eye closed. 'Is this because Charlie Notts is coming round?'

'What? Er, no! Why would that have anything to do with it?' I hope my face hasn't gone bright red.

'If that's true, then why is your face bright red?' Paul's not helping.

'Forget about it, if it's going to make you two go all conspiracy theory on me.'

'Oh my God, no!' Jenny is up and holding her bag and racing towards me like a big-boobed gold-hooped flash of lightning. 'This is going to be so much fun. And I thought today was going to be another lame-o day with you two.' Paul doesn't know how to take that one, so he just uses my grunting trick. Jenny is in full flow. 'I have always wanted my own makeover show.' She's tipped out the contents of her make-up bag on the floor. 'And what could be a blanker canvas than Gwendolyn Lewis?'

She pulls me up from where I'm sitting and eyes me like Picasso eyeing *his* blank canvas. Or like a baker eyeing his ingredients. Or perhaps like a cat eyes a cornered mouse.

'The thing is, Gwynnie, you are not as ugly as you try to be.'

'Er, thanks.'

'Skinny is in.' She looks at me in my cut-off tracksuit bottoms and football top. 'But you have to know how to use it. Have you got any tight jeans or smock tops?'

'Smock whats?'

'Well, anyway, you don't have them here do you? No, right now we'll have to make do with what we've got.'

'How long is this going to take?' Paul asks. Now he knows how I feel when he spends the afternoon with his tongue down Jenny's throat.

Jenny and I both ignore him. 'Let's start with your eyes. You have grey eyes that you need to emphasize to enhance their beauty and give you that wow factor.' She spreads out the fingers of her hands when she says *wow*, as if she was a sorcerer. 'The most important part is the eyeliner, because that will really make your eyes stand out.'

She rifles around in the pile of cosmetics and finds the thing she's looking for. It's a black pencil like the one I used on my lips that time, but now I realize that it's for the eyes. I am actually learning something from Jenny Gregson. The question is, is she really going to help me or will she make me look like a panda who hasn't slept for three days?

'Now just relax,' she says, and she sounds like a surgeon. I'm scared, but the way she holds the pencil, it's like she's so completely familiar with it — like the way I hold an Xbox control pad, or kick a football. She knows what she's doing, and that makes me relax.

She draws a line around my eyes and I realize that eyeliner does exactly what it says on the tin.

'Where's the mirror?' I ask.

'Na-huh. Not yet.' She wags her finger at me like I'm a naughty child.

She gets out something else. I'm pretty sure it's mascara, but what do I know?

'Now this, Gwynnie, is called mas-ca-ra.' She says it like she's teaching a language.

'Thanks, Jenny. I do know what mascara is.'

She shushes me by putting up a hand. Clearly I'm in the presence of the master here and I mustn't dare to interrupt. She twists open the top and pulls out a circular brush like the one I poked myself in the eye with the other day. 'Close your eyes.' She swipes at my lashes a bit. 'Now open them . . . I said, open them!' She has lost her surgeon cool for a second. 'Now look up.' She does her thing, working her magic and finally she says, 'Now look at me.'

When I look down again Jenny's face is right up close to mine. I flinch. But she smiles at me in a way that she's never smiled at me before:

genuinely. And do you know what? It's quite nice. I can't help myself but smile back.

'There you are,' she says. 'That's already an improvement. What do you think, Paul? Don't you think that Gwynnie looks almost pretty with mascara on?'

Paul has taken advantage of the fact that Jenny isn't demanding his attention and he's playing *Pro Evolution Soccer*.

'Paul!'

'What?' He doesn't even look away from the screen.

'What do you think?'

'Yes,' he says, still not looking.

But Jenny seems pleased enough by that. 'See, even Paul notices the difference, and Paul never notices anything.'

She's referring to the time when she had half a millimetre cut off her hair and he didn't say something about it. She didn't speak to him for like two hours. Personally I think that would be a relief. But I'm not going to be mean about Jenny any more because she's acting really sweet. I think it's more for her enjoyment than mine, but still, she's helping me. It's not like she's going to try and remove my eyeballs or anything.

She looks for another thing in her bag and pulls out the scariest object I've ever seen. It's definitely an eyeball remover! It's silvery metallic with handles like scissors and it's got a crushing mechanism.

'What's that for?' I ask, completely terrified. Yes, she still looks like she knows what she's doing, but now she looks like a butcher, or a psychopath, and I'm *not* her first kill.

'It's an eyelash curler.'

'You are not coming near my eyes with that thing!' I'm yelling for my life here and putting my hand up to block her.

'Gwynnie, if I'm going to do this makeover then you just have to trust me. Do you trust me?'

Er, no!

'Of course I do, Jenny.'

'Good, then here goes. Close your eyes.'

I close my eyes for what I imagine must be the final time. Shame that the last thing I'll ever see is Paul playing Xbox while picking his nose.

She clamps the thing around my eyelashes and says, in a way that I know she means it, 'Don't move!' I don't even breathe. Eventually she releases my left eyelashes and starts on the right.

'There,' she says like Picasso again, putting the final touches to her painting. 'Now look in the mirror.'

I'm pleasantly surprised! I definitely look better. It's as if my eyes are twice the size they were before.

'They look great!' I say. 'Jenny, what did you do?'

Jenny looks really proud of herself, and for once she deserves it.

'Thanks so much,' I tell her.

'You're welcome, Gwynnie. Right, next, we're going to straighten your hair.'

At this point Paul looks up from his game and stares at me. 'Gwynnie, you look different.'

Is that good or bad? 'Do I look OK or do I look stupid?'

'You look different.'

I don't know what to say. Paul has never complimented me on anything other than my football skills or a move on the Xbox or something. If that *was* a compliment, it feels weird. But he goes back to his game so I don't have to say anything.

'I told you I was a miracle worker. If I can improve someone like *you* this much, imagine what I could do to Angelina Jolie or Penelope

Cruz.' She picks up the straighteners that she apparently carries with her everywhere.

'Do you know what Jenny?' I say. 'I don't think I can handle having my hair straightened today. What's that phrase about running before you can walk?'

'You shouldn't do it.' She's made a joke and I smile at it.

'Exactly. I think I'll leave it at the eyeliner, macs-ra-ra and curled eyelashes for now.'

'OK,' she says. 'But this has been fun. If you ever want make-up lessons, give me a call. I've been doing it since before I ate solid food.'

'Cool. Thanks.'

The way we look at each other makes me think that we are actually friends.

Somewhere below the earth, hell freezes over.

chapter 10

The doorbell rings and Angela yells that she will get it. It's Charlie Notts. My heart starts beating really fast and I feel a bit ill. I grab the controller and demand that Paul and I play a two-player so that I won't have to talk to Charlie.

Charlie sort of knocks on the door and then opens it. He looks a bit shy because he's never been to Paul's house before.

'Hi, guys.'

'Heya, Charlie,' says Jenny.

'All right, mate,' says Paul.

'Hi, Gwynnie,' says Charlie. But I'm too embarrassed to look up so I just say, 'Hi,' and carry on staring at the screen. I'm glad that this make-up looks good but I don't want him to think that I've made an effort or anything.

'Nice pad.' Paul's got a ginormous plasma screen TV that looks wicked when you play

Xbox and really comfy brown leather sofas. 'Are you playing *Pro Evo*? Can we put on *Gears of War* after? I've never seen the new one. I've heard it's great.'

'It is,' says Paul. 'I'm pretty OK at it. Gwynnie's the expert.'

'Is that right, Gwynnie?' Charlie asks. 'Will you give me a demo?'

Paul stops the game and hands Charlie his controller. For one second I think that Paul is trying to be a brilliant host, but then he says, 'Well, now that Gwynnie has someone to play with, me and Jenny are going to go to my room for a bit.' He walks over to where Jenny is sitting and gives her a hand. She takes it and he pulls her up and kisses her properly on the lips — tongues and everything. 'Come on, Jenny.'

She squeezes Paul's bum to make sure that we know what they will be getting up to next door. 'Bye, guys. Don't do anything I wouldn't do . . . which isn't much!' She giggles and they leave the room.

It's just me and Charlie, we're sitting next to each other on the same sofa and suddenly I wish I had never suggested that he come over. I have no idea what to do. I mean, I speak to blokes all the time, like Paul, and Ranj, but it's usually to say, *Pass it!* or, *Did you see the match?* or, *You're such a knob!* I've never had a proper conversation with a proper bloke.

I keep looking at the screen when I say, 'Want to play *Gears* then?' I stick the game in the machine, not waiting for an answer.

'Yeah. Cool. Whatever,' he says.

Charlie is definitely feeling a bit awkward too, perhaps because I still won't look at him. He says, 'So, is it better than the first one?'

'It's OK.'

That killed that conversation so I try something else. 'Here, you have this controller. That one doesn't really work. But I know how to make it work because I've used it loads and . . .' I realize I'm sort of rambling so I just stop speaking mid-sentence, which is worse than rambling because it sort of brings attention to the rambling and makes it more obvious that you were rambling in the first place . . .

I'm doing it again.

'Thanks,' he says, and takes the good controller.

'What's properly cool about this game is you can use your partner's body as a human shield.'

'Ooooh, that's wicked! I am so going to use your body as a human shield!'

'My skinny little body wouldn't be much of a shield, Charlie. You might as well hold up a toothpick in front of you.'

Charlie laughs and says, 'Don't put yourself down, Gwynnie. I wouldn't call you a tooth-pick – a pencil maybe, but not a toothpick.'

He's joking so I throw a pillow at him. 'That's so rude!'

I laugh. Oh my God, I am talking to Charlie Notts and we're laughing together! OK, he's laughing *at* me, but still. I don't know much about blokes, but I've heard that it's a good thing when they insult you.

'The truth hurts,' he jokes, and he looks at my face properly for the first time. Then he says, 'Oh,' like it just slipped out.

I quickly wipe my nose and check it for bogies. 'What?'

'Nothing.'

Has he noticed my make-up? Does he think it looks good or does he think it looks rubbish? 'What?' I ask.

'Nothing.'

I smile at him. 'You're just trying to put me

off my game, but I've got my eye on you, Charlie Notts.'

'And a very pretty eye it is too,' he says, and winks at me.

I've gone a bit shy now. I shuffle round a little so he can't look at me.

Fffbrrrrrp.

Oh my God! The movement of my skin against the leather sofa has just made this really bad farting noise.

'Pardon you,' he says.

Just when it was all going so well! It's our first time alone together and he thinks I've farted in front of him. 'That wasn't me!' I say, and I know I am as red as a baboon's bum. 'I didn't just fart. I swear!'

He's smirking. 'If that's true, then why are you blushing?'

'It was the sofa. I moved on the sofa—'

'Millions would believe you, Gwynnie, but I don't. Call me cynical . . .' He's shaking his head in disappointment.

'I don't fart, not ever!' Then I realize that I might be protesting too much. 'I mean, of course I *fart*. Everyone farts. But not in front of people, only when I'm on my own and—'

He's laughing at me properly now. 'OK, OK, Gwynnie!' he says through his tears. 'You fart, but only for your own personal use – I get it.'

I decide to fight fire with fire, laughter with laughter, fart with fart. 'If you don't believe me then . . .' I shuffle my body on the sofa again, but this time for longer and more slowly.

Fffbrrrrrrrrrrrp.

'Good one!' he says. I've impressed him. 'Let me try.'

Fbrp.

'Pathetic,' I say. 'You've got to really push down and then slide along.'

Ffbrrrp. 'How was that?'

'Better,' I say. 'Like six out of ten on the Richter scale. A slight rumble, but you're not going to bring any buildings down.'

He leans over and drags his arms across the leather sofa. *Fffbrrrrrp.* 'What do you think? Might take down a garden shed, I reckon.'

I laugh. 'It needs work.' With all our movement we're sitting even closer than we were before. I give him a *Ffffffffbrrrrrrrrrrp,* just to show off.

He's nodding his head in approval. 'OK, I bow to your leather blow-off prowess, but I bet you can't beat my armpit farting extraordinaire!'

He puts his hand under one arm and brings the other arm down fast.

Bppprrrrfllllp. Comes from his armpit.

Is there anything this boy can't do? 'Wow!'

I try the same and put my hand under my arm. *Bprflp.*

'Not bad, not bad,' he says. 'Try cupping your hand a bit more.' *Bppprrrrfllllp.* He shows me.

'Oh cool!' I try again, using his brilliant cupping technique. *Bpprrflp.*

'Good!' *Bppprrrrfllllp. Bppprrrrfllllp. Bppprrrrfllllp.* He's flapping his arm like a demented, one-winged chicken.

I join in. *Bppprrrrfllllp. Bppprrrrfllllp. Bppprrrrfllllp.*

We're flapping and farting in unison. I bring in the leather farts to the mix. *Bppprrrrfllllp. Fffbrrrrrrrrrrrrp. Bppprrrrfllllp. Fffbrrrrrrrrrrrrp. Bppprrrrfllllp.*

He flops over towards me because he's laughing so hard. 'Gwynnie, you're so—' Our heads are about a millimetre away from each other.

I interrupt him with a *Fffbrrrrrrrrrrrrp.*

He laughs again.

'What's going on?' Jenny and Paul have just

walked back in from the other room and they look completely perplexed. Which only makes me and Charlie laugh harder.

'We could hear you from next door.'

'Hahahahahaha!'

Jenny looks disgusted. 'What the heck are you two doing?' she asks.

'We're starting a band,' I say, through the tears. 'The Loud and Prouds,' and Charlie looks like he's in pain.

'I didn't know you could play an instrument, Gwynnie,' says Paul.

'Stop!' cries Charlie. 'Please stop!' He grabs my arm as if he might fall off the sofa. Then he does fall off the sofa and he pulls me with him.

Jenny scowls as she looks down at us. 'You two are weird.'

I don't care if I'm weird. Charlie's weird too and we're rolling round on the floor together. We're just two weirdos that fancy each other like crazy.

*

Two hours after Charlie Notts and me were rolling around the floor together I realize that there is no way he will ever fancy me the way I am. This happens when me, Charlie and Jenny are all standing outside Paul's house about to go home. Charlie says, 'Hey, Gwynnie, I don't have your number.'

OK, it's not the completely romantic way that I'd hoped he'd ask for my number, but he's still asked for my number.

He gets out his phone. 'Call me and I'll save it.'

'Er, I don't have a mobile yet.' This is why I need a mobile phone. Mobile phones were invented exactly for moments like these.

'Oh.' Charlie, like everyone, is shocked by this fact.

Jenny cuts in as if she's trying to be helpful. 'It's OK, Charlie, Gwynnie can always get you on my phone.'

'Nah, that's cool,' says Charlie. 'I'll take your home phone.' He starts tapping at his keypad. 'Hang on a sec, I'll add you to my "Mates" group.'

Charlie Notts has just said that I'm his mate! This is fantastic. I wonder if he means *mates* like friends, or *mates* like mates on nature shows.

He gives me his phone to type in my number. There don't seem to be any girls' names in his phone. This is great! I am the only girl who Charlie wants in his phone.

Hang on a minute. Doesn't he have Jenny's number?

'Do you want to enter Jenny's number after I put in mine?' I ask.

'I already have it,' he says.

'But it's not here,' I say.

Something about the way Charlie sort of blushes and looks at the floor tells me that I'm not going to like what I am about to hear. 'No, er . . . this is my "Mates" group. I put Jenny into my "Girls" group.' Jenny beams, but when Charlie turns to look at her she drops the smile. 'Sorry, Jenny, I hope you don't mind.'

Jenny nods in a kind of forgiving *that's OK* kind of way.

I am destroyed. Charlie doesn't think of me as a girl. He thinks of me as a mate! And obviously not a nature-show-type mate.

'I can put you in under "Girls" instead, Gwynnie. If you like.' He grabs the phone off me and gets to the Girls group, then hands the phone back to me.

I am astonished at how many girls he has in his phone. It just makes it all the worse that he doesn't think of me as one of them.

'Whatever,' I say, and type in my number.

'Anyway, see you at school tomorrow.' I give him back his phone and run away from them, not able to even say goodbye.

Maybe if I was more ladylike then he wouldn't just think of me as a mate. Maybe Kevin's right: I have to act more like a girl if I want guys to notice me.

Will it work? Maybe it won't. I'll have to give up football and Xbox and start hanging around with all those stupid BB girls. But then again, it would be so amazing to be Charlie's girlfriend, to kiss him, to go out on dates and stuff.

OK . . . That's it . . . I am going to do it.

Gwynnie Lewis is going girlie!

chapter 11

'Honey, you look gor-geous!'

We're at the bus stop and everyone hears Jenny's screech. First they look at her. Then they look at me. Then they all start looking at each other and whispering.

Rewind three hours:

I get up stupidly early, have a shower and wash my hair. My hair takes ages to dry but luckily I've got Mum's old hairdryer so I set it to high, aim it at my head, and sort of shake it around like I've seen women do on adverts.

But when I look in the mirror it's not like the adverts at all! My hair's gone frizzy and mad. I need straighteners to fix it. Trouble is, I don't have straighteners. Then I realize, I do have an iron.

As I run the iron over my hair I hear this sizzling noise. And what's that burning smell?

'Ow ow ow ow ow ow!' I've singed the top of my ear!

When I look in the mirror I see that the straightening hasn't gone well. Half my hair is like Neanderthal woman, and the other half is straight, but emitting smoke. Not a good look.

To try and hide the frizz I put it in one of those high ponytails the BB girls sometimes wear. But unfortunately the ponytail reveals my left ear, which was burnt by the iron, and the tip is blistering like a heel after playing football in new boots.

Oh well. Next: back upstairs for make-up.

I'd better start with my eyes as, although they were closed when Jenny did them, I think I know what to do. I find the black pencil and try to draw a straight line around my eyes. A four-year-old could have done a neater job, but it certainly brings out the definition and gives them the wow factor.

I get out the mascara and try to swipe it along my eyelashes. But I seem to miss my lashes and get it all over my eyelids. I have to spit on my finger and rub it off – which just smudges the eyeliner. Still, it looks okay from a distance.

Now for the terrifying bit: the eyelash curler.

I bring the big scary object to my eye, clamp it around my lashes and squeeze. Just as I have the contraption holding firm, my dad shouts up, 'Gwynnie! It's nearly time for school!' and the shock of his voice makes me jump and I pull out nearly half my eyelashes!

'Ohgodohgodohgod!' It really hurts and I automatically rub my eyes as they start to water. I now have make-up all over my cheeks as well as my eyelids, and half an eye that's completely bald. But there's no time to do anything about it so I just plaster on more make-up.

I don't know what colour lipstick to choose so I go for the brightest red that I have.

It's really, really red.

Lastly I get the skin-coloured powder and use this fluffy brush to put it all over my face. The brush feels really nice and I get a little carried away.

But I've messed up again! The skin-coloured stuff has gone all over the stuff I've already done. This gives me two options: take it all off and start at the beginning, or put more make-up over the top.

I go for option B.

Next problem: clothes.

Like I said, I don't have any skirts. I do have one dress, but it's the one that I don't want to talk about. And even if I did have a skirt, I wouldn't wear it. My legs are so skinny they could be blown away by a slight draught. So instead I find a pair of Levi's and a shirt to wear on top.

One last look in the mirror and I take a deep breath. With the corners of the shirt I make a knot so that I'm showing my belly.

More importantly, my belly-button.

And now I'm here at the bus stop, three hours later, and everyone is looking at me wondering who I am and what the flan has happened to the real Gwynnie Lewis.

'You look so good.' I can't tell if Jenny's being honest, or being nice. Or maybe neither.

'Hi, Jenny.' I just about get the words out.

'Is this because of the lesson I gave you yesterday?' She's still speaking really loudly. 'If you want, I'll give you some more coaching after school, to teach you properly.' She can see my worried look so she quickly adds, 'Don't get me wrong – you look fabulous! I'm just saying that it's not easy when it's your first try.'

79

I hope no one can see how red I'm going under all this make-up.

'And why have you been hiding your divine little stomach under all those gross T-shirts and sports clothes?'

'Erm.'

'From what you're wearing, I'm guessing you want me to get you into the BB Club,' she stage-whispers. I nod. 'I can get you in, no sweat. It is basically *my* club after all!'

I don't know if I feel like a supermodel or a five-year-old, but I let Jenny lead me over to the BB Club because I am totally out of my depth here and she is slap bang in the middle of her depth. The BB girls are standing in their usual space: leaning against the railings of Becket's Park.

I can see Charlie Notts up ahead and we have to pass him to get to the girls. I'm praying that we won't have to talk to him, but Jenny makes sure that we do. 'Heya, Charlie, look at Gwynnie. Don't you think she just looks awesome?'

I've got shooting pains all up and down my left arm: the first sign of a heart attack.

Charlie says, 'You look really nice, Gwynnie.'

Charlie Notts thinks I look *really nice*. I act

completely gracefully by replying, 'Hwah, phn-ma, sllmp.'

Jenny starts laughing at me, but not in a mean way, just in a kind of *isn't my friend Gwynnie so silly sometimes?* way. 'Oh, Gwynnie, you're an absolute riot when you're shy around boys!'

Charlie says, 'Gwynnie's not shy around me, are you, Gwynnie?'

'Hsma, waa, ngag,' I say, coherently.

'Besides,' he says, 'she has nothing to be shy about. She looks good.'

Charlie Notts said that I look *good*! I don't give a damn if this heart attack kills me, my life is complete. It couldn't get better unless I was signed for Tottenham.

'She *does* look good, Charlie, you are right,' says Jenny. 'And I don't care what anyone says, but over-applying the make-up is brave, and some people can even pull it off.'

I was worried about the make-up, but Jenny is making this out to be a good thing.

'The critics might disagree, but size zero is still so in right now,' she continues as if evaluating some piece of modern art. Wasn't there an artist who tried to pass off elephant dung as a masterpiece? That's what I feel like right now.

'Well,' she says, 'Gwynnie is more like a double zero, which is even better. Most guys say they want girls with a bit more meat on them. What do you think, Charlie?'

Whatever Charlie says now is going to be the most important thing he ever says ever. He will either finish me off, or make me float.

'I couldn't possibly comment on what *most guys* want, but I think Gwynnie looks very nice today.' He looks at me and says, 'Not that you don't look nice every day, Gwynnie. I'm just saying, make-up suits you.'

That's it, I'm airborne.

'Are you going to talk to Paul?' he asks. 'I want to see if I can borrow one of his games.'

I didn't see Paul arriving at the bus stop. I am worried what he'll say about how I look, but I also want to spend every second with Charlie, so if Charlie is going to talk to Paul then I am too. 'Yeah, of course—'

'Er, no!' Jenny cuts in. 'Gwynnie is coming to talk to my friends over here. Gwynnie and Paul are not joined at the hip, you know!'

'Yeah, Charlie,' I say. 'Me and Paul are not joined at the hip, you know!'

Jenny drags me away and we leave Charlie stranded.

'You're welcome,' says Jenny, and I don't know what I'm welcome to. 'I purposefully steered you towards Charlie so that he could see how nice you look. But top tip, sweetie: always leave them wanting more. If they want to spend time with you, that's when you leave.'

Jenny is going to teach me so much about being a girl.

We get to where the BB Club are standing and I feel almost as nervous as I did when I was approaching Charlie Notts. Jenny takes the lead. 'Heya, ladies, how's it going?'

They are dumbstruck.

'Don't stand with your mouths open, you might catch flies,' she says. 'Gwynnie wants to be in the BB Club and I think we should let her.'

Kimba pulls her bitchy face, which she does so often it's become her normal face. She looks me up and down and says, 'She doesn't have her belly-button pierced, so she can't. Sorry, Gwynnie.' She doesn't look sorry at all.

'But,' Elizabeth Phillip says really quietly, 'Tanya doesn't have hers done and neither do I.'

'Yes, thanks for that, Elizabeth,' says Jenny,

frowning at her as if she's interrupted an adult conversation. 'Kimba, the BB Club has always been about a shared ideal.'

'But,' says Melissa, 'as Gwynnie herself once said, we don't want to include even more members that haven't got their belly-buttons pierced. People might start thinking we're idiots.'

I have to fight back the urge to say what needs to be said. Yesterday's Gwynnie wants to kick Today's Gwynnie's in the bum. But Yesterday's Gwynnie wasn't called *really nice-looking* by Charlie Notts, so who gives a flan about Yesterday's Gwynnie?

'Actually, Gwynnie was quite rude about the whole thing,' says Melissa.

'What's with the long memories, girls?' asks Jenny. 'How about this? How about we give her, like, a bronze membership, like not a full membership, until she's proved herself?'

'Gwynnie?'

It's Paul. If anyone is going to full-on laugh at me without even trying to hide it, it's him. When he sees my face he literally does a double take. 'What the . . . ? What's going on, Gwynnie? Are you in a play or something?'

He's with Ranjit and Charlie, and Ranj is

equally shocked. 'Is this for a joke or a bet?' asks Ranj.

No one's speaking and I realize that it's up to me to save my own neck. 'Oh, Ranjit, you're too immature to understand the mind of a woman, and I haven't got time to explain it to you.'

Everyone laughs and Ranjit looks a bit sheepish. I feel bad for making him look stupid, but it seems to have done the trick and the BB girls are smiling at me. I am going to have to be careful that I don't turn out like Kimba. I will never be mean again.

'Paul, dollface,' says Jenny (*dollface?*), 'can us girls just have a teensy minute to ourselves?'

'No probs. Come on, Gwynnie.'

So Paul doesn't think I'm a girl either.

'I'm going to stay and chat with them.'

'Er, OK. See you in a bit.' He looks confused.

As soon as the boys are out of earshot Jenny starts whispering to the BB Club. 'See, Gwynnie is what this club needs. She knows all the guys and they just come up and talk to her. They never just come up and talk to us.'

'But she's so sad-looking. She's missing half her eyelashes!'

It appears they might have noticed the

eyelashes. This is getting really embarrassing, but I want to be Charlie's girlfriend so much that I would take a thousand insults and pull out all my eyelashes to have him.

'Look at that shirt,' says Melissa.

'And no one wears Levi's any more,' Kimba helpfully points out.

'And there is something weird going on with her ponytail,' says Tanya, perhaps noticing the crazy frizzy burnt section of hair that's only half hidden by the straight section.

'Face it, she's not cool enough.' Kimba's made up her mind.

Jenny steps in. 'I'm going to help her work on that,' she says. 'And she's already come so far.'

If only they would be nice enough to talk about me behind my back. I pretend I'm not there and run through my make-up routine as if it was a football set piece. *Powder to cover face. Eyeshadow marks eyelids. Eyeshadow to eyeliner. Eyeliner to mascara—*

'OK then,' says Melissa.

'OK then, what?' Pretending I'm not here means that I haven't a clue what they're talking about.

'OK then, we'll allow you into the club.'

'Only on a bronze membership though,' Kimba says, clearly not convinced.

'That's great! Thanks so much!' Suddenly I realize that sounds a bit desperate. 'I mean, yeah, OK, whatever.'

Paul shouts over to me from where he's standing with the other boys. 'Gwynnie, we can't be bothered to wait for the bus. We're going to jog up to school and get in a game of footy. You coming?'

All eyes are on me. What do I say? 'Errrr.' Then I put on this girlie sort of pout and say, '*Footy? Jog?* No, thank you! I might break a nail.'

The BB girls smile. I've done well.

'Er, OK. Catch you later, yeah?'

'I'll pencil it in to my calendar.'

The BB girls are now beaming at me. I roll my eyes at them as if to say that Paul is such a muppet sometimes. I'm becoming a mean girl and I hate myself a little bit. I won't do it again and I make a promise to apologize to him later.

But now I'm a BB girl. Next stop: Charlie Notts's girlfriend!

chapter 12

My dad comes in the front door whistling a Spurs tune and carrying a takeaway pizza. We haven't had pizza in ages because Dad says we can't afford luxuries these days. Doesn't he understand that pizza isn't a luxury, it's an absolute necessity.

We're eating in silence, which is OK by me, until my dad makes a noise that sounds like he's just stubbed his toe, but with his mouth full of pizza. He has dropped a pepperoni slice on to his chin. It looks like a nasty scab. I can't help but laugh. He brushes it off his chin and there is a big red greasy patch underneath. I laugh even more.

Dad goes, 'Bmdompn't flaughfff.' He's still got a mouthful of pizza.

'Sorry, Dad, I can't understand you with your mouth full.'

He swallows his food and he's laughing too.

'I said, don't laugh! That burnt my chin.' He's smiling at me. It's been a long time since my dad's been happy, so I'm happy too. 'Imagine that, a father who has burnt his chin off.'

'I'd still be seen with you, Dad . . . I'd just make you wear a bag over your head.'

'Thanks a lot.' He knows I'm joking.

He lets the silence fall again and I know what's about to happen. The fun and games were just to ease me into a false sense of security before he starts . . . *talking*.

'So . . .' he says, 'I hear you've made some new friends.' How does he know that? Has he been spying on me?

'S'pose.' I am desperately hoping that something will happen to stop this conversation before it starts. Like maybe the phone will ring, or the house will fall down.

He sort of clears his throat and continues, but in a serious way. 'Now listen, Gwynnie, it's only natural for your taste in friends to change at this time in your life because there are a lot of other – erm – changes going on for you at the moment.'

Oh God, please don't let him say the word that every girl hates to hear. He actually mouths the sentence to himself before he can bear to speak it out loud.

'Ahem. You are going through – erm . . .' even with practice he can't do it without stuttering, '*puberty*.'

That's it! That's the word. It's not so much the word itself but the way adults say it. They either sort of whisper it like it's a secret word that only teenagers and embarrassing parents know, or they say it like it's just a normal word and not the most embarrassing thing ever.

'You will start – er – periods, and – er – boys.' He's having just as much trouble getting this out as I am hearing it. 'When a man and a woman are in love, often they want to – erm – do things together—'

'We don't need to talk about this,' I say, throwing him a lifeline.

'You might not want to talk about this now, but some day you might have some questions you need answering.'

What does he think the Internet is for?

Dad's mumbling his way through his speech, emphasizing the important words: '. . . Pregnant . . . Wear A Condom . . . Diseases . . . Sexual Intercourse . . .' He's making the same face as when I've seen him clean dog poo off his trainers. But trying to do it with a smile, which is so much worse.

'Dad, I know it all already.'

He looks horrified. 'You know it *all* already!?'

Oh God, now he thinks I am the most experienced girl this side of White Hart Lane.

'What I mean is, we have education classes at school.' I leave out the word *sex* as I can't say *sex* in front of my dad. I realize that *education classes* doesn't really make sense, but it's the best I can do.

'I know, Gwynnie, but—'

'It's cool, honestly.'

'It's just that, with your mother gone . . .' He hesitates for a sec, as he always does when he mentions Mum, and I hate it. I hate it that he misses her as much as I do. 'You might think you have no one to talk to. I want you to know that you can always talk to me – about anything—'

'That's great, Dad, thanks.' Quick, change the subject. 'Is there any football on tonight?' But he's stuck on *puberty* like Claudio Gentile marking Diego Maradona.

'I've spoken to Angela and she said that you're welcome to talk to her if you'd like.'

'You've been speaking to Angela about me?' So that's how he knows about my *new friends*. Angela must have told him about Charlie and Jenny.

'I speak to Angela about lots of things.'

I imagine this Gwynnie convention with charts and pictures of me while they all discuss what's going on with Dad's weirdo daughter.

'I'd better go, Dad. I've got homework.'

'Well . . . But . . . OK.' He admits defeat. 'Take more pizza if you want.'

'Thanks, Dad,' I say, and grab three slices out of the box.

I am just about to escape, opening the door with my elbow as my hands are full, when he captures me again. 'Gwynnie, just a sec . . .'

Not more puberty talk, please.

'I've got a job,' he says.

This is brilliant news. 'Dad! That's so cool!' I beam at him. It *is* really cool. 'Now we can have pizza every day!'

He laughs. 'Well, perhaps not every day. It's not a great job. I'm only working in a sports shop in the centre, but at least now we'll have a bit of money coming in.'

I'm so happy that I put my pizza down for

a second and go over and give Dad a big hug. 'Well done, Dad.'

He gives me a big hug right back. I love my dad sometimes.

'The best thing about the job is that I get a staff discount.'

Why is that the best thing about his job? Oh no, I can see where this is going.

'On Saturday we could go and get those football boots you wanted.'

Wanted. Past tense. I don't know how to tell him I'm not playing football any more. I say, 'We could wait a bit, Dad. Or we could not get them at all. You probably have other things you need to buy first, don't you?'

'There is nothing more important than getting my little girl her birthday present.'

I don't know how to tell him that I am not into football any more. Maybe I won't have to. Maybe the shop will burn down before then. Maybe they'll put a nationwide ban on football. Maybe, if I'm really lucky, my feet will fall off.

*

It's Saturday morning and all I have done this week is speak to girlie girls on Instant Messenger or Facebook or both at the same time. We can have, like, a two-hour conversation about rubbish, but mostly we seem to talk about Charlie Notts, which is a subject that never bores me.

Elizabeth P says < wot do u think he wears in bed? >

Tanya D says < definitely plum burgundy silk pjs that his dad bought him when he was on a diplomatic trip to japan >

Melissa R says < no way! he wears boxer shorts 2 bed and the tight ones 2 so u can c the outline of all his bits >

Elizabeth P says < lol >

Tanya D says < lol >

So I quickly write < lol > too.

Jenny G says < u lot r obsessed! itsa bit sad really >

Elizabeth P says < imagine pulling them off. like unwrapping a present 2 c the 'package' inside >

Jenny G says < lol >

Kimba O says < lol >

Tanya D says < lol >

So I write < lol > too.

So far with the BB Club I have bided my time. I don't say too much in case I get anything wrong. But I can't keep quiet while they talk any more — especially as they talk so much!

Gwynnie L says < i bet he sleeps naked! lets just spend a moment thinking about that . . . >

Kimba O says < yum yum >

Elizabeth P says < mmmmmmm! >

Tanya D says < he definitely sleeps naked >

Elizabeth P says < hey gwynnie, we r meetin at s bucks to talk more charlie. u wanna come? >

Paul S says < hi. wanna play g of w l8r? >

I'm about to answer his message when Jenny pings in with. < we cd go shopping and get G some new clothes! that wd be awesome! >

Elizabeth P says < cool. makeover! >

Kimba O says < i spose that might be ok >

Tanya D says < primark here we come! >

Melissa R says < usual time usual place? >

I have no idea what the usual time or place is. I'll have to call Jenny. Everyone agrees. Then Melissa goes:

Melissa R says < wot were we talking about? o yeah. charlie notts naked . . . >

'Gwynnie?'

So there I am, I've basically created an online forum about naked men, and my dad has sneaked up behind me.

'What are you doing?' he asks.

'Nothing. Just talking to my friends.'

'Why has someone just written the words "takin off ur bra"?'

'It's just my friends being stupid.' They must be running through the *how far would you go with Charlie Notts* conversation.

'These friends are not older men, are they? You haven't arranged to meet any strangers, have you?'

'No, Dad.' Parents always think their children are so stupid. I cover the screen with my hand. 'Do you want something?'

'We're going to get your football boots, aren't we? I'm ready when you are.'

Errr.

'We can get some lunch too, if you like.'

My dad is being so nice and it's making me want to be nice back. But I don't need boots any more, and I *do* need clothes.

'Actually, Dad . . . I don't think I want those Nike Mercurial Vapor VFGs made from Teijin synthetic leather that adjusts to the contours of your foot.'

Dad looks really confused. 'What do you mean, Gwynnie?'

I stare at the floor and mumble, 'I want to spend the money on something else.'

'What do you want to spend the money on, Gwyndoe?' My dad looks really worried, and for a second I think it would be funny to say, *A boob job*. Which actually might be an idea.

'Um, I think I want to buy some new clothes.' I don't know why I feel bad when I say this, but I do.

'What do you need?'

'Umm . . .' I don't know how to tell him.

'Do you want to buy a – erm – bra thing?' My poor dad. If we have to have another embarrassing girl conversation I think he might combust. 'I've heard that Marks & Spencer is a good place—'

'No!' I've got to stop him before he says the words *cup size*. For both our sakes. 'No. I want to spend it on clothes . . . at Primark . . . with my friends.'

'Oh, OK. No problem.' Dad looks crushed. He takes out his wallet and hands me a wodge of notes that is more money than I have ever held in my entire life. 'Of course you don't want to go shopping with your old dad.' He is trying to not sound sad, but he's not doing a very good job.

'Sorry, Dad.'

'No, no. You go and meet your friends and have fun. It's your birthday treat. I've got things I need to get done today anyway.'

'Thanks so much, Dad.' My dad is officially the best dad ever.

So I am about to go shopping with girlie girls. I have no idea what to expect.

chapter 13

Shopping is the most exhausting sport in the world. It tests strength, stamina, endurance and even mental agility as some of the clothes require a PhD in mechanics to work out how to do them up.

'Gwynnie, you just have to try this.'

'Gee, you'll look so good in this.'

'Try this one on in a 10 and an 8 and see which is better.'

'This would *so* go with that goooorgeous little thing over there. You just have to try them together.'

They pile stuff into my arms and it's heavier than a thirteen-year-old boy. I know that because we once did an experiment to see if I could pick up Paul. This hurts worse than that as I have to hold the clothes as we do multiple circuits round the shop.

'Try this.' Jenny puts a flowery shirt on top of the pile. 'The pattern's not very nice, but just try it.'

'Errr, why am I trying it if it's not very nice?'

They stop in their tracks and look at me like I'm insane.

'Because things sometimes look different once they're on,' Melissa tells me. 'Haven't you ever been shopping before?'

Thinking about it, I'd have to say, *Not really.* Whenever I've needed a new T-shirt, or tracksuit bottoms, or socks, I ask my dad for the money, he gives it to me, I walk into the shop, pick up the thing in the right size, pay for it and leave. I've never done *this* before.

I'm in a cubicle trying to work out whether the long tube is supposed to be for my arm or my leg. I look on the tag for clues. Fortunately it helps me out; it says 'Off-the-shoulder top'. OK, that's a good start, but why, if this tube is for my arm, is there only one of them? Primark must make tops for people who have had an arm amputated in an accident or something. I shout over the wall, 'Do they make clothes for people with disabilities?'

'Oh, Gwynnie, you have issues, sure,' Jenny

shouts back, 'but I wouldn't say you had a disability.'

'I don't know, does lack of dress sense count as a disability?' I can tell that's Kimba being mean, but I ignore it.

Maybe this isn't an armhole at all. Maybe it's supposed to be one of those *accessories* I have heard so much about. The top goes off-the-shoulder, so I put it round me under my armpits and across my chest. But where does the long tube thing go? It must be at the back, like a tail. It wouldn't be at the front like an elephant's trunk; *that* would be stupid!

I quite like having a tail to swoosh.

'I think I am going to get this one,' I say.

'Let'sseelet'sseelet'ssee!'

I pull back the curtain, proudly showing off how good I look in my new top.

They all stick their heads out and crack up laughing.

'Oh, Gwynnie! You are hilarious!' Tanya says.

'Don't you like my tail?' I ask, feeling confused.

'A tail!' Jenny says through tears of laughter. 'Good one, Gee.'

I pretend it was a joke and laugh my head off

too but I have no idea why. I stand in my cubicle for a moment and feel confused. A moment later there's a patting against the curtain and I realize that it's someone trying to knock.

'Gwynnie?' It's Elizabeth. She's whispering. 'Can I come in?'

'Yeah,' I whisper back.

She sticks her head through the curtain and looks at me in my top. 'That top is really nice and the colour is nice too, but it comes in another colour that I think might work better for you. I got you one in your size.' She hands me the same top but this time in a dark grey. 'And, um, that's not how you wear it.'

I feel really stupid and try to shrug it off like I knew that all along. The shrugging makes the top fall down from under my armpits and I have to catch it before I expose my M&M boobs.

'You put one arm in the tube,' says Elizabeth, still whispering so the others can't hear, 'and the other side leaves your shoulder bare.'

'Oh.'

She must have seen the look on my face as she says, 'Don't worry, it confused me the first time I tried it.' Then she smiles and retracts her head back behind the curtain.

I reshuffle the top like she says, and I suppose it makes more sense. I show the other girls.

'I told you to try that one,' says Kimba. 'It was a good choice of mine.'

'You look fully awesome,' says Melissa.

'You're so lucky, Gee,' says Elizabeth. 'You have such a nice flat stomach.'

'That colour is exactly the same as your eyes and it really brings out their beautiful shade,' says Tanya.

'Thanks, Tanya.' Wow, I feel so good about myself.

'And doesn't Gwynnie have divine hair,' says Jenny. 'It's so long and lovely.'

They all nod in agreement.

This is such a surprise. They are being so nice it makes me want to be nice to them too.

So when Tanya shows us what she's tried on I say, 'Ooooh, that skirt has so many flowers on it!' I'm not sure if that's a good enough compliment, but Tanya seems to like it.

Then Kimba comes out in a dress she's tried on. 'That dress is completely pink. It really brings out the beautiful colour of your eyes.'

Kimba looks at me like I'm insane.

And to Elizabeth, who has only tried on

some bangles and a scarf, 'Your hair is really clean.'

She says, 'Thanks, Gwynnie,' with a big smile. And we all feel like proper friends.

Then I spot the tag. 'This must be a mistake.' I turn to the rest of the girls and show them. 'It says it's only three pounds.'

'That's Primani for you,' says Jenny.

When she says *Primani* they all laugh.

'Pradamark,' says Elizabeth, and they all laugh again.

'Primada,' Melissa says and they laugh more. I laugh at these nonsense words too, but I have no idea why.

Primark is, without doubt, the best shop in the world! With my £110 I have bought the whole place twice over. I buy jeans, leggings, jeggings, loads of tops and dresses to go over trousers and tons of accessories. I buy the off-the-shoulder top. Even if I did prefer it when it had a tail.

I now have a wardrobe full of clothes and shoes and jewellery.

And I am now a fully fledged girlie girl.

chapter 14

'Gwynnie! Phone!' Dad shouts up from the hallway.

'Who is it?' I shout back, already running down the stairs, hoping it's Charlie calling to declare his undying love.

'I don't know. Didn't ask. But weirdly enough, she sounds like a girl.'

I grab the phone out of his hands. 'Very funny.'

'I know!' he says, and walks off like a grinning loon.

'Heya, Gwynnie. It's Elizabeth.'

'Hi, Elizabeth, how are you? Did you need some help with the geography homework? Because I'm telling you—'

'No. Just calling to say hello really.'

This is weird. No one has ever called me to *say hello* before. 'Oh . . . hello.' What do you say after you've said hello?

'What are you up to?' she asks.

'Ummm. Not much. The phone rang, my dad made a rubbish joke, and now I'm talking to you.'

Elizabeth laughs. 'I'm bored. Want to come over? I've lost a few pounds this week and it might be fun to see if I could squeeze into something of yours,' she says. 'Fat chance – literally.'

'You wouldn't want to get into my stuff. I'm an extra small.'

'And I'm an extra large,' she says, sounding quite pleased about it. 'There must be a happy medium!'

We both laugh for ages about that and I think it might be fun to hang out with Elizabeth. But then I remember that I have plans with Jenny this afternoon.

'Actually, I'm going over to Jenny's. She says she's going to fix my hair.' I'd been thinking it will be a bit weird to go over to Jenny's just me and Jenny. It would be easier to have Elizabeth along too so all the girlie focus isn't on me. 'Want to come?'

'Do you think she'd mind?' Elizabeth asks.

'No, why would she?' Would she? 'I'll meet you there at twelve.'

*

It's about twelve thirty and Elizabeth and me are round Jenny's house, sitting in front of her mirror in her bedroom. There is something different about Jenny today, but I can't put my finger on what.

'So you gliiiiiide the straighteners down to the tips of your hair.' As she says *gliiiiide* she gliiiiides the straighteners. 'And now that bit is straight!'

'What?' I say, not quite believing that it's so easy. 'That's it?'

'That's it,' Jenny says.

'Wow.'

'Pretty cool, eh?' says Elizabeth. 'It's like an electric miracle!'

I smile at Elizabeth's joke, but Jenny frowns at her like this is not the time for funny. Elizabeth shuts up.

'Now you try,' Jenny says.

'What?' I feel like I am being asked to fly a plane with no training.

'You are going to have to learn so you can do it at home on your own.'

'But I don't have straighteners at home.'

'You could use an iron and an ironing board,' Elizabeth says, and she and Jenny start laughing.

'Yeah, what kind of idiot would do that?' Jenny says. I am exactly that kind of idiot. 'No, really, hon. You can have these ones.'

'What? Why?' Jenny is being so nice to me and I can't believe I was ever mean about her ever.

'We can't have a member of the BB Club going around looking ugly. No offence, Elizabeth.' Elizabeth looks crushed, then smiles, which makes it worse. 'Anyway, these are my old ones. I have some ghd's now so I don't need them.'

'What the hell are ghd's?'

Both Jenny and Elizabeth give me the *you have so much to learn* look, which I do, I know. 'They are, like, the next generation in straighteners and they are the best.' She hands me her old ones. 'These are nothing compared to ghd's, but they'll do.'

'Thanks so much, Jenny.'

She says, 'What are friends for?' Then she grabs me and gives me a big hug. This is weird. Apart from that time I scored the winner in the eighty-second minute, I have never been hugged by a friend before. It feels nice. I hug her back.

Suddenly she looks at Elizabeth. 'Elizabeth, sorry,' she says, 'I didn't tell my mom you were coming over as you came over uninvited, so there won't be enough lunch for you. Would you mind leaving?'

Elizabeth looks crushed again. 'Sorry, Jenny. Of course. I'll go.'

I feel bad for Elizabeth. 'I don't mind not eating,' I say. 'I could go.'

'No, no, it's fine,' says Elizabeth as she grabs her bag and runs out the door. 'See you later, you two. I'll give you both a call in a bit.'

'Yeah, whatever.' Jenny shuts the door on Elizabeth.

I frown at Jenny. 'That was a bit harsh, Jenny. I wonder if Eliz—'

'Gwynnie,' Jenny interrupts and looks wide-eyed and excited. 'I have an idea. Why don't we text Charlie?'

'Charlie Notts?'

'Of course Charlie Notts.' She looks at me like I'm some kind of muppet. 'Let's ask him if he wants to come to the cinema with us later.' Without waiting for my approval, she starts tapping away. She already knows what I'll say.

'And Paul?' I ask.

'Of course Paul.'

'What are you writing?'

'Oh, you know . . .'

I have absolutely no idea.

She presses send and we wait, without saying a word.

In a minute he's texted back. I grab for the phone but Jenny won't let me see it.

'He says he's coming!' she says.

'Oh my God. Did he say that he liked me or anything?'

'No. But he knows it's going to be just the four of us and he still said he'd come.'

'That's like a double date! I am going out with Charlie on a double date. This is amazing!'

'Well, yeah, but don't get too excited. It's still early days.' She looks quite serious and suddenly I get suspicious.

'What does it say exactly?' I grab for her phone. She tries to stop me, but I am too quick for her. I ignore the puke-inducing photo of her snogging Paul on the screensaver and get to her messages. When I see the list of messages there are actually quite a few from Charlie, but there are loads from Paul and the other BB Club members, so I just check the last one. It says:

cool will b gd to c u x

'He hasn't mentioned me.' He hasn't even

mentioned Paul, and Paul's Jenny's boyfriend. 'What's going on, Jenny? Does Charlie fancy you?'

'Don't be silly. "u" means me *and* you *and* Paul. You two are totally implied in the message. Who else would I bring along besides my boyfriend and my best friend?'

Wow! Did Jenny just call me her best friend? Does that mean I have to say she's my best friend?

'So, do you think he wants to see me then?'

'Of course he does!' This must be why Jenny sent Elizabeth away; she's setting me up with Charlie Notts. If that's not a best-friend thing to do, I don't know what is! I feel a bit bad for Elizabeth, but she'll understand when we explain.

'Right,' she says. 'We're meeting in two hours outside the cinema and you've still got crap hair, which can't happen.' She gets to work on my hair again. Clearly there is no time to let me do it myself in this emergency situation.

'Er, Jenny, how do I talk to him?'

'What do you mean?'

'When he's around everything I say sounds so stupid.'

'You're right,' says Jenny, and she makes a face like this is *another* emergency that she needs to sort out. 'OK, two tips for talking to boys. First, always ask them questions about themselves and things they are interested in. They love talking about themselves. Second, if you can't think of a brilliant answer to something they've said, just laugh. It makes them think they're funny even when they are idiots.'

'That's genius!'

'I know. Also . . .' she continues. She loves giving me these lessons. 'You have to flirt as much as you can with other guys to make the guy you like jealous. If you can kiss someone else in front of them, that's even better. Basically, boys are obsessed by sex, so if you let them know that you're willing to do stuff, then they'll fancy you more.'

Does that mean that I have to snog someone else before I can snog Charlie Notts? That's going to be even harder than just snogging Charlie Notts.

'After your hair we have to do your make-up properly.'

'Shouldn't we text Paul first?'

'Oh yeah!' she says. She texts Paul.

'And maybe Elizabeth, to explain.'

'I'll do that later.'

I'm sitting there imagining my totally amazing date that I'm about to have with Charlie and I ask Jenny what her ideal date would be.

'Well,' she doesn't even pause; she clearly thinks about this stuff as much as I do, which is a relief, 'he would obviously have made a big effort. I hate these guys who just roll out of bed and think that will be enough to impress. He would have slicked back his hair so he looks all smart and be wearing a really cool designer suit. He'd arrive with a gigantic bunch of roses and give them to me with a poem that he had written himself saying how much he loved me and how amazing I am and everything. Then he'd ask the band to play *our song* and he would scoop me up in his arms and kiss me tenderly in front of everyone, so that they would know I was the only woman in the world for him . . .'

We both go all dreamy for a second just thinking about this scenario.

'Paul would be so sweet if he did that for you.'

'Paul?' It's like I've woken her out of her dream and she has to remind herself who on earth Paul is. 'Oh yeah, Paul. He would be so sweet doing all that.'

She sort of changes the subject by going to her drawer and getting out these slimy pink things that look like raw chicken and stuffing them in her bra. I knew there was something different about Jenny when I arrived: her boobs weren't as ginormous as they usually are. Now that she's put the slimy things down there, they look massive again.

'What the hell are they?'

'Chicken fillets.'

'Ewww. Won't they go off?'

'Are you always this dumb, Gwynnie, or do you put it on for show?' She chucks me one and I try not to show how repulsed I am by the thought of touching it. They feel gooey, and when I take my fingers away I'm amazed that my hands aren't covered in sticky stuff.

She continues to explain. 'They help enhance the size and shape of your boobs. The trick I use is to put three fillets in each cup.'

'You stuff your bra?'

'Not *stuff,* en-hance. It's totally different.'

She's says it's different, but I'm not sure that it is.

chapter 15

Charlie sat next to me at the cinema. At one point he put his arm on the back of my chair. But when I leaned back so that he basically had his arm around me he apologized and took his arm away again. I giggled, like Jenny had told me to, but Charlie just gave me a weird look.

Still, there is no denying that Charlie and I just went to the cinema with another couple. I'm sure that means that we are a couple. Nearly.

After the cinema we all sort of hang around outside for a bit. Paul and Jenny are holding hands and I keep changing my position so that Charlie can hold my hand if he wants to. He doesn't though, but I suppose that he is not ready to go public with our relationship yet.

'Do you guys want to come back to my house?' Paul asks.

'Yeah, all right,' I say. I am probably not

allowed to play *Gears of War* now that I'm a girlie girl. What the flan *are* girlie girls allowed to do? I guess that's why we're always phoning and IMing saying how bored we are.

'Um, sorry, hun,' says Jenny. 'I've got to go back to mine. My mom's got this stupid thing where she wants us to spend time together as a family, so we're having this big ol' sit-down dinner.'

We all groan and feel sorry for her. What's with parents always wanting to spend time as a family?

I say, 'Yeah, dudes, actually I think I best go home too.' *Dudes?* Why did I say that? No one says *dudes.* I cover it up by quickly saying, 'Paul, are you coming, dude?' as if *dude* is coming back and I'm not a weirdo, I'm more of a trend-setter.

Paul looks at me like I'm a weirdo.

But then Jenny says, 'Where do you live, Charlie?'

'Near Mount Street. Do you know it?'

'Well golly, what a surprise! I live near Mount Street too.'

I'm sure she already knew that.

'I could walk home with you.' Charlie quickly looks at Paul. I think he's checking it's OK. I guess

he's realized that Paul is the only proper friend he's
made at Northampton Hill High, and even though
he's not in the same year as him he doesn't want to
lose him as a mate.

'That would be real swell of you, Charlie,'
says Jenny, and looks at Paul like he better not say
anything. 'Paul's not the possessive type, thank
God. I just couldn't stand it if he was.'

Paul can do nothing but nod and smile at
Charlie.

'Does Gwynnie live near you, Paul?' asks
Charlie. 'Can you make sure she gets home safe?'

He cares about my safety. That's a good sign.

'Yeah, she lives round the corner.'

Paul doesn't need to sound so disappointed.

'Nice one then. You can walk Gwynnie home
and I'll walk Jenny home. See you at school,
guys,' he says. 'See you, Paul.' Charlie and Paul
do that eyebrow-raising thing that blokes always
do that says goodbye without having to smile.
'See you, Gwynnie.' He leans forward. He's
going to snog me! I sort of stand there like a
lemon and wait to see what I should do. I get my
lips ready and open my mouth a bit in case he
puts his tongue in. He presses his cheek against
my cheek and sort of kisses the air by my ear like

I've seen the Year 10s do. He's so mature! I'm hoping that it's just a kiss on the cheek before he goes in for the big snog . . . But it isn't. He just steps back and smiles at me. At least I can say that Charlie Notts has kissed me.

Jenny comes over to me and says, 'Bye, Gwynnie,' and does the same thing as Charlie just did. When did we start kissing each other goodbye? Just then, I suppose.

Paul gives Jenny a proper snog, and Charlie and I have to stand there like knobs while they go at it. It's like Paul is one of those people who put a towel on their sunlounger so no one else lies on it. Paul is saying to Charlie, *Jenny is my sunlounger, and you better not lie on her*. They finally stop snogging and she says, 'Come on then, Charlie, let's go.'

Paul and I watch them walk off together. Paul's frowning. He calls after her, 'Make sure you text me to let me know how rubbish your dinner is!'

She sort of waves a reply without looking round. She's too busy giggling at whatever Charlie just said.

Paul and I start walking back home and what's weird is that it's really weird between us. For the first time in my life, I have no idea what to say. I'll do that question thing Jenny suggested. 'Did you see what Victoria Beckham was wearing to the Gucci party?'

He looks at me like I'm talking the alien language we just heard in the movie, only without subtitles. 'Er, no.'

'She looked ridiculous.'

'Oh.'

We walk along in silence again before Paul gives conversation a go. 'Did you see Lampard's free kick?'

'No.'

'I know you hate him, but that kick was something else. From way outside the penalty box.'

'Oh.'

'And what about Spurs beating Newcastle?' he says. 'You must be well chuffed.'

'I didn't see it,' I say. Somewhere inside me my heart squeezes in my chest and I realize that I miss Spurs like an old friend.

'Oh. Well, you should have. It was a good game.'

Instead of thinking about how much I miss Spurs, I concentrate on why I'm doing all of this. 'What do you and Charlie talk about when me and Jenny aren't there?' *Please say me. Please say me.*

'Not much. Football mostly.'

'Oh . . . Does he ever talk about me?'

'No. Why?'

'No reason.'

This is the worst conversation I have ever had ever.

'Hey,' he says, all excited again, 'Ranjit's arranged a match against some of the kids from Queen Charlotte's Grammar after school tomorrow.'

'Why the hell was Ranj talking to the kids from Queen Tartlet's?' I ask. 'Is he doing research on what makes people act like knobs?'

Paul laughs. 'No. It was wicked. Ranj was wicked.' Paul turns to me and his eyes are all wide and excited. 'There was like twenty of the Tartlet kids all hanging around the bus stop—'

'*Our* bus stop? What were they doing there?'

'I don't know, but anyway . . . They were all hanging round at the bus stop thinking they were cool or whatever, when they see us coming, so they start acting all loud—'

'Idiots!'

'I know. One of them takes out a cigarette and

he goes to Ranj, *You got a light, mate?* and Ranj is like, *No. I've got a life, mate, so why don't you jog on.*'

'Good one.'

'Well, it sounded cooler than how I just said it to you now. Anyway, they started saying how Northampton are rubbish because we've got a rubbish pitch.'

'Which is true,' I say with a shrug and a nod. 'It is a rubbish pitch.'

'I know. But they're not allowed to say that. Anyway, Ranj was like, *We have the skills to play on a pitch that has a few bumps in it. You posh kids need everything ironed out by your butlers.*'

'Brilliant.'

'He tells them how they don't want to get their dainty boots dirty so they have to play on AstroTurf.'

'I bet they didn't like that.'

'Then I say, *Come on then, let's have a match. That is, if you don't mind getting your ♫ shoes mucky ♫!*" and I sort of sang *"shoes mucky"* so they knew that we thought they were girls.'

'They *are* girls!'

'So then they had to agree to play against us. It's tomorrow after school. Can you come? You're our best winger.'

What can I say to that? I put it simply. 'I can't come.' There is just no way. I guess this is what they mean when they say you have to make sacrifices for love.

'Why not?'

'Jenny and me and the others are going into town to get frappuccinos.'

Paul stops talking and frowns. He can't look at my face and I know this is where he asks me what's going on. He mumbles something under his breath that I can't hear.

'What?' I ask. But I don't really want to know because it won't be good.

'You never want to play football any more.'

I say nothing.

'You've gone all weird.'

'I don't know what you're talking about,' I reply.

'You're all frappuccinos and manicures these days. You never want to kick the ball around the park or come over and play *Pro Evo*. Why not? How come you suddenly don't like this stuff?'

He's getting angry with me. So I get angry with him for being angry with me. 'I don't know why I don't like those things any more. Maybe I have just grown up a little bit and you haven't. Girls mature faster than boys—'

'That's such a load of crap! *Girls mature faster than boys!* Just because you ponce around at Starbucks all the time, bitching and gossiping about people, doesn't make you mature. Especially as I know you don't like coffee.'

'I love coffee actually.' I can't stand it. But the mochaccino is OK if you ask for an extra shot of chocolate and whipped cream on top and add loads of sugar.

'No, you don't, you hate it. Why are you acting like a muppet?'

'I'm just acting like your precious girlfriend Jenny Gregson. You don't say this stuff to her.'

'Because you're different to her.'

I'm not sure why, but that comment makes me the angriest of all. 'Maybe I'm not different. Maybe I am exactly the same.'

'You're not. You've changed.'

I think about that for a second. There's nothing I can say. It's totally true. 'You changed first,' I mumble. But luckily he doesn't hear me.

chapter 16

'OK, children, I have some good news and some bad news.' The Dazzler is chuckling away so we know that both will be bad news. 'The good news is that the board has made their ruling. School uniform is going ahead. Effective immediately.'

Everyone goes into a state of shock. The place is silent. Like we can't quite believe it.

'Your teachers have already given you a list of acceptable attire, and I expect to see you all wearing it tomorrow.'

'Oh my God!' Elizabeth whispers to me, although she needn't have whispered as everyone is talking.

Tanya, who is sitting on the other side of me, says, 'We'll look like those posh kids from Queen Charlotte's!'

'That would be the worst!' says Elizabeth, nodding.

'Don't worry about it,' I whisper back. 'Jenny says that it's just a threat. They can't actually make us do it if we don't want to.'

Elizabeth doesn't look convinced but Tanya nods and looks happy again. Tanya can be like a puppy at times – one minute she's whining and the next she's wagging her tail. Not literally, of course.

'OK, quieten down now.' The Dazzler is trying to get us to shut up. 'I have to tell you the bad news: we have decided to allow a school prom to go ahead.'

Now everyone gets really excited. Elizabeth squeezes my arm and Tanya gets into full-on puppy mode – she squeals and looks like she's about to pee.

'What we need is a group of volunteers to organize the event.'

All the BB Club look down the row at each other and nod an agreement: we are the people to organize this prom. We are the only ones who could make it cool. Jenny sits up a little and catches Melissa's eye, sitting behind us with the Year 10s. They nod at each other and everyone in the school sees. This is going to be the BB Club's prom.

*

'We should start with the most important stuff,' says Kimba, 'and then work back to the least important.'

We all agree. We're taking this very seriously. We've brought notepads and pens and files to Elizabeth's house after school for our first official BB Club Prom Planning Committee meeting. Macaroni – Elizabeth's fluffy Pomeranian dog – is also sitting in the circle with us as if he's contributing. But he's not. Unless you call bad breath a contribution.

'So,' Kimba continues, and looks at the list on her paper, 'when shall we have it?'

Elizabeth stands up, grabs a calendar from her wall and flicks through the pages. 'Um, May is always nice,' she says.

We all shrug, like, *OK, why not?*

'But can we do it at the end of May?' she asks. 'So that we have time to lose a few more pounds before then.'

That's hardly an issue for me, but they are all nodding and shrugging at Elizabeth, and even Macaroni is panting in agreement, so I nod along too.

'That's decided then,' says Melissa, 'Saturday the 30th of May.'

Kimba looks back at her list. 'More importantly than the date – what're you guys wearing?'

The girls all speak at once until gradually they work out how to take it in turns.

'I think I am going to wear this red strapless boob tube—' says Melissa, but she is instantly interrupted by Jenny.

'Er, like *all* boob tubes are strapless. Duh, Melissa!'

What's a *boob tube*? It sounds painful. I've heard of a pointed bra, but a tube-shaped one would be weird.

'I drew my ideal dress in art class,' says Elizabeth. 'But Mrs Gatwood took it off me and said that I wasn't paying attention. And I was like, *Hello! This is art class . . . I'm drawing.*'

'What are you going to wear, Gwynnie?' asks Tanya.

'Jenny said she'll straighten my hair with the ghd's.'

'But what are you wearing?'

'I don't know,' I say, and they all look at me like I am a disorganized freak. It's like they have been planning for prom their whole lives, when we just found out about it this morning. The only thing I can think of is something a Disney princess might throw on, but I don't think that's really me. 'Maybe leggings with a dress over it.'

'You can't wear leggings to prom!' They all shout at exactly the same time, then giggle a little.

'I know, I know. I was only joking.' I was not only joking. Lucky we're having this meeting or I would have looked like a fool.

'What about that one really pretty dress you have?' says Jenny.

'What dress?' I ask. I have no idea what she is talking about. I only have one dress and that's—

'You know . . . The blue one . . . The one that's hanging up in your cupboard downstairs.'

Jenny's only ever been in my house for about two milliseconds. Somehow she's managed to check out my cupboards.

'I'm not wearing that.' I would never wear that dress in a million years.

'Why?' asks Kimba. 'Is it even more hideous than everything else you own?'

'That dress is the most beautiful dress in the world!' I snap at her. It's more precious to me than a million signed photos of Gazza or a million Mulberry handbags. I could never fit that dress. And I don't mean because it's not my size.

'But, Gee, it's so—'

'I'm not wearing it, OK!' I sort of shout at Jenny. I have never shouted at Jenny. I don't think anyone ever has. Jenny pouts and everyone goes all quiet for a minute. I pray they are not about to chuck me out of the BB Club for being a bitch. Or reduce my bronze membership to wood. 'Sorry, Jenny.' I say.

Elizabeth speaks quietly to Jenny. 'It must be her mum's,' she says, and I well up a little because she's exactly right.

'That's OK, Gwynnie,' says Melissa. 'You can wear what you want.'

They all nod along, even Jenny.

'Let's change the subject,' says Tanya, and I'm really touched. Girls can be really nice when they want to be. 'Who do you want to snog?'

All of us say Charlie Notts. Except for Jenny, who will be snogging Paul all night.

'OK,' says Tanya. 'But none of us are allowed to be jealous if someone else gets to snog him.'

'We'll add a Charlie Notts non-jealous clause into the pact of the BB Club,' says Melissa with a nod.

'That, and that no one is allowed to buy the same dress,' adds Kimba.

'Well, I'm not jealous, obviously, because I have Paul,' says Jenny. I think she feels a bit left out when we talk about Charlie because she has already found the love of her life. 'It's our eight-weekiversary on Wednesday.'

'You've been going for eight weeks?!' Elizabeth gasps. 'That's like, for-ev-er. You two are such a good couple.'

Tanya opens her mouth wide. 'Do you think you'll get married?' she asks. 'Do you think he'll propose when you turn sixteen?'

'I don't know. Probably,' she says. She's thought a lot about this. I've seen the ring she's designed and everything.

I want to ask the BB girls about something. I wasn't sure before, but now that they are being so nice I say, 'Girls?'

I wait till I have their full attention. They know this is going to be good.

'If I tell you something, can we make it part of the BB pact that no one is allowed to say anything about it?'

Melissa looks me right in the eyes with the most sincere expression. 'Gwynnie, we would never tell anyone anything you tell us in confidence. That's, like, fully the thing that BB girls don't do.'

I wait a minute before I look round the group and say, 'How many boys have you ever got off with?'

'Four,' says Melissa.

'Six,' says Kimba, looking smug.

'One,' says Tanya, a bit embarrassed.

'Er,' says Elizabeth, 'there was that one time where it almost happened with Terry Phelps, but then his mum arrived to pick him up.'

Jenny comes in with, 'Well, I'm on eight,' like it's no big deal and we won't be impressed or anything. 'One party I was at last year I got off with three guys in one night. It was such a cool party.'

'I wish I'd been there.' Then I ask the thing I need to ask, 'How do you know when a bloke is going to snog you? How do you get a guy to actually do it?'

'Usually the guy is all over you,' says Jenny. 'At least, that's what happens with me. But sometimes they need a little help. You need to be in a position where they don't have to travel too much distance to get their lips to your lips.'

I imagine myself spending a whole night standing right in front of Charlie with our noses pressed together.

'So, like, when you're sitting next to a guy you have to snuggle up to his arm so he knows that you want him to put his arm around you,' Jenny says. 'Then you sit there for a bit and usually he will just grab you and snog you. But if he doesn't then you can sort of look at him for a second and lean in and see if he tries it.'

'Um, OK,' I say. 'But, what if he doesn't?'

Tanya asks me, 'How did it happen with that guy you snogged?'

This was a lie I told to the BB girls. I told them I kissed someone called Chris Waddle when I was on holiday with a long-lost cousin of mine from Newcastle. But, like Elizabeth, I've never snogged anyone. I can't bear to tell them the truth so I lie even more. 'That's the problem, I don't remember. One minute he was standing next to me and the next . . .'

'That's what it's always like!' says Elizabeth.

Kimba gives her this look like, *How would you know?*

I continue. 'It was so long ago I think I've forgotten how to kiss.'

Jenny looks really sorry for me and gives me a big hug. 'Oh, hun. It's real easy: firstly, you have to do it with your eyes closed. People who kiss with their eyes closed are more passionate people. I always kiss with my eyes closed unless I'm checking to see if Paul is kissing with his eyes closed.'

I nod. Eyes closed. Easy.

Then Melissa cuts in. 'His mouth has to be around your mouth because he's the man and the man's mouth has to be on the outside to show that he is dominant.'

Dominant is bad. OK.

Now Kimba's saying, 'Make sure that you don't move your tongue round and round his tongue, because then people will call you a dishwasher.'

'Don't just push your tongue in and out or else they'll say you're a pogo,' says Melissa.

'If you waggle it from side to side you're a windscreen wiper,' says Tanya.

They all make a *yuck* face.

'Windscreen wipers are, like, the worst!'

There's so much to remember!

'You have to vary it up a little,' says Jenny. 'A bit of normal kissing, like pecks on the lips. Then a staircase—'

'What's a staircase?' I ask.

'When it goes your top lip, his top lip, your

bottom lip, his bottom lip. So you are sort of sucking each other's lips.' When she makes the kissing face, Macaroni comes over and tries to lick her on the lips. Jenny just manages to push him away before she gets snog number nine.

'OK,' I say. 'That makes sense.' I'll have to skip the staircase.

'But never do one technique for more than ten seconds at a time or else the kissing gets boring and the guy is just waiting for it to end,' Melissa says.

'Did you hear about Lucy Bellings in the year above?' asks Kimba. 'She made Robin Hall fall asleep when she was kissing him. She didn't even notice for about ten minutes until he started snoring in her mouth!'

They all laugh, and now I'm even more nervous.

After the meeting Jenny and I are walking home and she turns to me. 'You never really snogged that guy on holiday last year, did you?'

I have to think about whether or not to confide in her. Then I remember that she is my best friend. 'No, I didn't.'

She goes quiet. I feel bad. Like I've betrayed her.

'Sorry, Jenny. I didn't mean to lie to you, but I'm just a bit embarrassed about it. You won't tell anyone, will you?'

She looks me straight in the eye. 'I don't understand why you felt you had to lie, honey.' I think she is going to get angry but then she hugs me. 'I won't tell anyone. I promise.'

'Thanks, Jenny.'

'What are best friends for?' she says. And I think that best friends are for exactly this.

chapter 17

Kevin's car is outside the house when I get home from school today. Nice one. I haven't seen Kev in a while.

He must not have his whippet ears in because neither Kev or Dad shouts hello to me when I close the front door.

Dad's saying, 'I don't want to put you out, Kevin.'

Then Kevin says, 'Dad, I swear, it's fine. I got a little extra this month.'

Is Dad borrowing money from Kevin?

'You don't need it to take out this new girlfriend of yours?'

'Really, Dad. I said it was fine last time.'

Dad's borrowed money from Kevin before?

'Honestly,' Kevin says, 'Gwynnie is more important.'

Dad's borrowing money from Kevin for me?

I burst into the kitchen and, sure enough, Dad is shoving some notes into his pocket quickly so that I don't see, but I do.

'Hi, Gwyndoe. I didn't hear you come in.'

'Hi, Dad. Hi, Kev. What are you doing here?'

Kev rolls his eyes. 'Charming, isn't she? I've come to see my geeky Dad and my spotty sister. Is that all right with you?'

I run and check my face on the microwave. No sign of a spot. Then I remember that Kevin's always called me his spotty sister.

'I am not geeky!' Dad says, pretending to be offended. 'I bought the latest Katy Perry CD, I'll have you know.' Dad thinks he's so down with the kids because he's heard of Katy Perry.

Kev says, 'But you have to admit that my sister is spotty.'

'Oh yeah,' Dad replies. 'I can't argue with that!'

Those two are about as funny as an episode of *Songs of Praise.*

'How's Paul, Gwynnie?' asks Kevin. Kevin hearts Paul. I sometimes think that he wishes Paul was his brother rather than having me as his sister. 'Is he still going out with Stephanie Gregson's little sister?'

'Yeah, it's their eight-weekiversary today.'

They both laugh as if young love is the most hilarious thing since their hilarious double act from a moment ago. Kevin says, 'Oooooh, did he get her something nice? If fifty years is gold, what's eight weeks? Dust? Hot air?'

'I don't know. Maybe I could ask him if I had a mobile phone.'

Dad and Kevin look at each other and smile.

'Did you want a mobile phone, Gwynnie?' says Dad. 'You should have said something.'

'Senility is clearly setting in early.'

'So you don't want this phone I got you?' he smirks.

What?! 'Did you get me a mobile?'

He nods. Kevin nods too. Dad pulls out a box from where it's been sitting on a chair pushed in under the kitchen table.

'Dad, you're the best dad ever!'

He hands it to me and I take it out of the box and look at it. It's a pretty cheap model but it's the latest cheap model, and it's the same one that Melissa has, but in black, which is really cool. I put in the SIM card and battery, and plug it in to charge.

'Don't you need to read the instructions first?'

'No one reads instructions, Dad,' I say, getting out my book with all my friends' numbers and tapping away at my phone.

'Yeah, Dad,' says Kevin. He's taking the mick, but I don't care.

I text Jenny:

hey Jenny, its gwynnie. i hv finally got a mobile! its a rubbish model but at least i'll b able 2 txt u now ☺ tb x x

Jenny texts back:

cool. i can bore u with my problems 24/7. lucky u ☺ x x

I text:

when do u think i should txt cn? tb x x

Jenny takes about ten minutes to tb, as if she's really thinking about it:

I wd wait til he asks 4 ur number dont txt him b4 he asks 4 it

I text:

wot? not even 2 tell him i hv a phone?

Jenny texts:

NOT EVER!!!!!

I know Jenny is right about everything to do with boys, but the whole point of me getting a phone is so I can text Charlie Notts. I have to do it. I put it as if I've texted it to everyone.

I text:

hi everyone. this is my number if u wnt 2 txt me.
make sure u do. gwynnie x x

I then text Jenny to let her know what I've done:

Sorry but i had 2 do it. i just sent cn a txt. it said
hi everyone. this is my number if u wnt 2 txt me.
make sure u do. gwynnie x x do u think i sound like
a muppet? tb

Jenny tbs:

ur an idiot! make sure u do sounds soooo desperate.
have u already sent it?

Oh God! I *have* already sent it! It does sound desperate. It sounds more sad and desperate than when Sarah Louri told Asher Quinn that she loved him in a poem that she read out in English class. I am never going to live this down! Charlie Notts is never going to talk to me again. I am always going to listen to everything Jenny says from now on.

I text:

o god! ive sent it. am i more desperate than sarah
louri?

Charlie tbs:

hey gwynnie, u finally have a phone. how cool.
welcome 2 the 21st century. u will find emergency

exits here here and here. lol. just obeying your
orders to tb. tb x x

Oh. My. God! Charlie Notts has just texted
me! He didn't think I was sad or desperate.

I text:

cn just txt me! omg! he told me to tb. wot should I
do?

Again, Jenny waits about ten minutes before
she tbs. She's putting a lot of thought into this:

wow! if hes replying 2 desperate msgs like that then
mayb hes desperate 2 and u and him and sarah
louri can make a desperate people club. woteva u
do dont txt him back

I wait twenty minutes with the phone in my
hand and then I text Charlie again. I know Jenny
said I shouldn't but I can't help it:

sorry 2 send u a txt with orders, im practising 2 b a
sergeant major lol. but ill nvr do it again. u no im a
complete nutbag x x

CN tbs:

ull nvr send me a txt again? ok. u will nvr hear from
me either. i did no u were a nutbag. now i hve it in
writing. don't tb ☺ x x

Oh Goddddddddd! I have completely started
and stopped all textual conversations with Charlie
Notts in one go. Why did my dad have to buy

me a phone? It's ruined my life in less than an hour.

I text Jenny:

i have accidentally just told cn 2 never txt me again.
help!

Jenny tbs:

lol! only u cld do that G. uve blown it now. i cant
help u x x

I tb:

wot if i invite him to Julie innis's partee? i cld ask him
2 come 2 urs 1st? tb x x

Jenny tbs:

it wont work. uve blown it. don't worry we'll find u
sum1 else x x

But I can't believe I've blown it. I can't leave it there.

I text Charlie:

r u going 2 julie innis's party? we r. do u want 2 come
with us?

CN tbs:

my doctor has told me that im allergic 2 nutbags.
but ill make an exception, as its u x x

I text:

omg he's coming! wot should i wear?

CN tbs:

defo smart /casual ☺

What the flan have I done?! I have sent the wrong message to the wrong person and now Charlie will guess that I have a tiny little crush on him. Right, I'm throwing this phone away now.

It rings before I can bin it. It's Jenny.

'Hi, Je—'

'What's going on, Gwynnie? I just got a text from Charlie saying he's meeting up with us before Julie's party.'

'Yeah, I asked him and he said yes. Isn't that—'

'He said *yes*? To *you*?'

'Yes. He said he'd come only *as it's me.*'

She goes all quiet for a bit and I think I might have offended her by not doing what she told me to. 'Sorry, Jenny, I know you said—'

'It doesn't matter,' she says, but it sounds like it does matter a little bit. 'See you tomorrow at school.'

'Wait a minute,' I say. 'Isn't today your eight-weekiversary? Where's Paul?'

'Oh, he's here.' She doesn't seem like she's having a great time. They were supposed to go to Nandos, but the lack of background noise means they can't have. 'Look, Gee, I've got to go.'

'Gwynnie . . . !'

I have only just noticed that my dad and Kevin are no longer in the room. My dad is calling from the front door.

'Gwynnie, I'm just popping round to see Angela. Back in a couple of hours.'

When did my dad start spending so much time with Angela?

'Kevin!' I call out.

'I'm off too!' he shouts back, and the door slams behind him.

'Jenny?'

But Jenny's hung up.

I text Elizabeth:

hi Eliz, its G. i gotta fone. This is my numbr so u can call me whenevs

Elizabeth tbs:

that's soooooo cool! txt cn and c if he txts back. do it now, b4 u lose ur nerve!

I can't tell her that I've already done that, and it didn't exactly go well.

chapter 18

Jenny and me are talking about Charlie, as usual, as we get ready for Julie Innis's party.

'Has Charlie been texting you?'

'Yeah. A bit.' He's texted me a couple of times this week. I'm so happy. 'And he always puts kisses on the end of the texts.'

This makes Jenny go really thoughtful, like she hadn't expected it. 'Do you think he likes you?'

'I don't know. I'm hoping something will happen at the party tonight. I am going to try your leaning trick.'

Jenny's still thinking, and then suddenly she smiles and says, 'What are you wearing?'

'Well, I'll definitely wear chicken fillets.'

Jenny laughs. 'I meant what *clothes*! But thanks for sharing.'

'Oh,' I say, and go red. 'Well, obviously I'll be wearing that really nice blue top that—'

'No. I think you should wear the yellow one.'

'But Kimba said that I can't pull off yellow. I don't have the colouring and it makes me look washed up.'

'But yellow is, like, your best colour! She's trying to stop you wearing yellow because you look so good in it.'

I should have known Kimba was lying. She pretends to be nice to me, but I know she hates me. Luckily I brought it, just in case. So I get it out of my bag.

'Oh, and btw,' Jenny adds, 'the phrase is washed *out*.'

Oops.

'And when are you going to finally get your belly-button pierced?' she asks.

The thing is, I don't want to get my belly-button pierced. It will definitely hurt, and, well, I don't want to hurt myself on purpose. 'The thing is,' I say as I pull the yellow top over my head, 'my dad will definitely ground me if I get my belly-button pierced. And, well, I don't want to get grounded or I might miss prom.'

'Okaaaay. But just so you know, you might miss out on certain privileges if you stay only a bronze member of the club.'

'Like what?'

'I don't know,' she says. 'We haven't decided yet.'

She leaves me with that bizarre thought as we head out to meet up with Charlie.

*

Kimba and Melissa are sitting on a wall outside Julie Innis's house as me, Charlie and Jenny walk over.

'Hi, guys,' I say.

'Hi Gwynnie,' says Melissa. 'Nice top.' She and Kimba look at each other and laugh.

'Thanks!' (I think.) 'Where's the others?' I ask.

Kimba frowns at me like I'm an idiot. 'Tanya can't come because her mum is really strict and won't let her do anything – everyone knows that.'

'And Elizabeth won't leave the house until she has lost a few pounds,' says Melissa.

'Probably for the best,' said Jenny.

'Definitely for the best!' Kimba says. 'We don't want another incident like sports day, Year 5.'

I remember sports day, Year 5. I won the running race that year and beat most of the boys' times too. But I remember hearing something about Elizabeth wetting herself.

'But that was ages ago,' I say.

'So?' says Kimba, with a mean look.

'What happened on sports day, Year 5?' asks Charlie.

Kimba laughs and says, 'Elizabeth—'

'Oh no,' I say to Kimba. 'Charlie doesn't need to know.' Elizabeth would be mortified if she thought that Charlie knew about the Incident.

'He'd be the only person in school who doesn't,' says Kimba. 'Besides, like you say, it happened ages ago.' She turns to Charlie with wide eyes – the look that she always gets when she has gossip. 'On sports day in Year 5, Elizabeth peed her pants! And as she was only wearing a gym skirt there was no way of hiding it!' Melissa and Jenny start laughing really hard. 'The Dazzler had to walk her back to school and she had to wear knickers from the lost-property basket. Yuck! – she really brings the BB stock down.'

'Honestly,' says Melissa, 'I don't know why we let her hang out with us.'

I can't believe they are being so rude about Elizabeth. 'Perhaps because she's really nice!' I say. 'So what if she peed her pants four years ago?'

Charlie smiles at me. 'Yeah, I almost peed my pants last week when I found out that Spurs were in the final!'

'Yeah, Kimba,' Jenny says to Kimba, who's suddenly stopped laughing. 'Anyway, talking of stock going down,' says Jenny, raising her eyebrows, 'did you not get in?'

'No,' says Kimba. No wonder she's so angry. 'But it's probably a lame party anyway. Don't know if I even want to get in.'

Melissa says, 'We tried knocking on the door but Julie said she isn't letting in anyone that isn't invited.'

'Well, we're still going,' says Jenny. 'Sorry, ladies, but when it comes to getting in places, it's every gal for herself.'

Charlie frowns, like he's not sure that it should be *every gal for herself.* He looks at Kimba and Melissa and says, 'I'll make sure she lets you in. We can't have you two sitting out here all night – that's if you want to come in.'

'Yeah! Thanks, Charlie!' says Melissa, and gives Charlie a smile so big he might have to apply suntan lotion.

'That's what I meant,' says Jenny, realizing that she might have sounded a little mean just now.

We all sort of stand back as Jenny knocks on the door. She looks really confident because she knows she's definitely getting in. Julie Innis opens it and looks at us like we are a smelly sock that she's just discovered at the bottom of her locker. 'What do you Year 9s want?'

Suddenly Jenny doesn't look so confident. 'Heya, Julie. How's it going? Can we come in?'

Julie's not sure.

'My sister Stephanie Gregson knows your brother's friend Ishi, and he said that you give awesome parties.'

Julie still looks doubtful. 'I've heard of your sister, but I don't know you. There's too many people here already.'

Charlie steps forward. 'Hi, Julie. Please don't relegate us to the league of saddos who couldn't get into the party.'

Julie melts like the Wicked Witch in *The Wizard of Oz*. 'Yeah, OK, you guys can come in, I suppose. We're playing Postman's Knock in a minute.'

Postman's Knock is where you spin the bottle

and then you have to spend two minutes in a dark cupboard with the person the bottle points to, kissing and stuff. She looks directly at Charlie when she says this and I know she's thinking exactly the same thing that I am: *I hope that I get put in the cupboard with Charlie Notts. And I hope they lock us in and throw away the key.*

Julie Innis's party is the coolest party ever, not that I've ever been to a proper party before. I have been over to Ranjit's house when a load of us watched *Terminator* and ate KFC, but I don't think that really counts. This is different. Loads of Year 10s line the corridor that leads up to the stairs and line the stairs too. I don't know what to say to them as it's doubtful they will know who I am, so I just do the eyebrow-raising thing but add in a smile. Sylvia Rontaller from Year 10 frowns at us like she has no idea what we're doing here, then checks out what I am wearing. The leer on her lips tells me she doesn't like it. I move on.

Looking at Charlie, I can tell that he's pretty uncomfortable too. 'Where shall we go?' I ask him.

The other BB girls turn to look at us; they want to be part of our plan, whatever it is.

'Head for the kitchen,' Charlie instructs us, like this is an SAS mission. 'We can get a drink and see if there's anyone we know in there.' We nod. That makes sense. 'If not, we can look like we just went in to get a drink, move on and reconvene in the garden.'

'OK,' says Jenny.

'We've got to stick together if we are going to make it out alive,' he says. 'No man left behind.'

'Roger and out,' I say, and Charlie smiles.

The kitchen is packed. It's only small but we could get a world record for how many people we fit in here. I see Estelle Cole talking to Foz Kassam and, as I once paired up with Estelle in a joint Year 9–Year 10 PE class I risk a 'Hi' and hope she remembers me.

'Hi, Gwynnie. Like your jeans.'

Wow, I wasn't expecting that!

'Primada,' I reply, and she laughs and Foz does too. This is going well so me and Melissa and Charlie stop and talk to them for a bit while Jenny moves on. I thought we were supposed to stick together.

'What's the party like?' Kimba asks. She tries to give the impression she has a million parties to go to tonight so if this one is rubbish she'll head off to another.

'It's really boring,' says Estelle, not really looking at me, her eyes moving round the room to see who else is here.

I look around; from an archway in the kitchen you can see into the living room. There are loads more people in there, all Year 10s and even some Year 11s. They have set up decks and there are loads of fit guys standing around them, looking at the records in the record box.

'Yeah, it's total pants,' says Foz. She's looking around too. I follow her eyeline to where Josie Mills is snogging Karl Purbeck. Foz smiles and whispers something to Estelle, who smiles and nods.

'How did *she* get *him* to snog her? He's a total hottie,' says Melissa.

There are two other people snogging on the sofa. One of them is Veronica Short. 'Who's Veronica eating over there?' I ask.

'Isn't that one of the posh kids from Queen Charlotte's?' says Foz.

'Social suicide,' says Estelle. 'She'll never live it down.'

'Well, at least she's snogging someone,' says Melissa.

'Yeah, but a Tartlet?' says Kimba. 'I'd rather snog my hand.'

Everyone wants to get off with someone – it doesn't really matter who, just as long as they do it so everyone else can see and as long as snogging them won't make them look sad. There is no one here that would make *me* look sad because, a) even snogging the saddest bloke in the world would be a step up for me, and b) they are all in Year 10 at least, which makes them automatically cooler. Oh, and c) I have never snogged anyone so I kind of just want to get it over with a little bit.

We leave the kitchen and head for the garden, following the mission plan. Jenny is already out there talking to the twins Susie and Sarah Bird.

'So me and my gals are going to make this the most awesome prom ever.' Jenny is saying this really loudly so that everyone can hear that it's the BB Club organizing it. 'I'm gonna get my hair fixed in town and I have already bought the most awesome dress. It's timeless and classy.'

'When is it?' asks Catherine Miele from Year 10. She's craning her neck to ask but she says it like she couldn't really care less, like if she's not doing anything else then she might fit it into her busy schedule.

'Two weeks' time. The 30th of May.'

Two weeks' time! Oh God. Something else is happening in two weeks' time and I can't believe I didn't realize before. All the boys in the garden start looking at each other, wondering if they will be able to come, and I know why.

'Like, what's the problem, fellas?' Jenny's noticed it too.

'Yeah, what's the problem?' I ask, but I know exactly what the problem is.

Peter Jameson says, 'That's the same day as the FA Cup final.'

Jenny rolls her eyes as if there is no contest between prom and the FA Cup final. And she's right, there is no contest – the FA Cup wins every time. I can tell that she's worried though. 'Prom doesn't start till half seven. Will that be late enough for you to make an appearance?'

'Yeah, the match finishes way before that.'

The female half of the garden breathes a huge sigh of relief.

'Well, you better be ready in time,' Jenny says. 'Don't want your dates to be kept waiting.'

'We need dates?!' Melissa shouts what we

were all thinking. 'When did we decide this? Why didn't this come up in the meeting?'

'Of course you need dates, silly. This is a prom. Don't you know anything?'

We all nod. Of course we knew *that*!

Jenny continues like she's giving a seminar. 'I know all about proms because I was in America this Easter. You have to have a date, and a dress, a corsage, and a limousine.'

Who am I going to get to ask me to the prom? It's too much to hope that Charlie Notts will ask me. Everyone in the whole school will want to go with him. (And what's a corsage? Is it a type of up-do?)

'Will there be a DJ or a band?' someone asks.

We panic. The BB Club spends the whole of our Prom Planning Committee meetings planning how we'll have our hair, who's going to snog who, what the posters will look like . . . we never thought about music and drinks and all that stuff.

I have an idea. 'My brother's best mate is a DJ in a club in town. He plays at Ministry of Sound in London sometimes.' This is true. Everyone is looking at me like I am the coolest thing since blue-flavoured slushie. I knew having a brother would pay off eventually.

Jenny looks at me and says, really nicely, 'Oh, don't worry, Gwynnie. My sister, Stephanie, knows loads of really cool DJs; I'll get her to find someone.' Suddenly I don't look so cool any more, but Jenny quickly says, 'Thanks though.'

Julie Innis announces that we are about to play Postman's Knock in the living room.

Charlie looks at me and winks. 'A Ministry of Sound DJ would be so cool.'

I catch Jenny looking at me. 'Yeah, Gwynnie,' she says. 'We should all go there some time. You know, if you think you could get in.'

*

Please let it land on Charlie. Please let it land on Charlie.

It's my turn to spin the bottle and I'm praying that it will land on Charlie so me and him will have to go in the cupboard and snog for ages. As the bottle turns I see Jenny look at her mobile phone for like the millionth time in the past twenty minutes. And that's a lot, even for her.

No one knows what happens when you are locked in the cupboard together, and the rule is you are not allowed to ask. But when Rosie Perry went in with Hamza Fenton we knocked on the door after their two minutes and they came out smiling and blushing. When Shelly Nettles went in with Guy Holloway they were still properly getting off with each other and we had to demand they come out. When Samantha Hill went in with Robert Mower they actually came out before the two minutes was up – Robert was basically running out of there. And when Mandy Palmer got Aaron Webb she actually refused to go in with him, which is totally against the rules, but she said we couldn't force her and I suppose she's right.

So the whole Postman's Knock thing could go either way.

Here I am, the bottle's spinning around and I am using up all my wish quota for the rest of my life to wish that it lands on Charlie Notts. If it does, I swear I will never ask for anything ever again.

I don't believe it . . . It's worked! The bottle lid is pointing directly at Charlie.

Please don't let him refuse to go in the cupboard with me.

chapter 19

'Come on then, Gwynnie!' Charlie orders me into the cupboard.

'OK, you two,' says Julie Innis. 'You've got two minutes.' She starts the timer before we're even in the room.

I have just two minutes in a dark room with Charlie to make him snog my face off and completely fall in love with me. No problem.

'Don't do anything I wouldn't do . . . which doesn't mean much.' She must have heard the same thing that Jenny heard about letting boys know you're willing to do stuff.

He opens the cupboard door for me and closes it behind him, leaving us in total darkness.

'Gwynnie?' he whispers.

'Yeah?'

'Do you think we should kiss?'

Yesyesyesyesyesyesyes. 'Everyone will think we're weird if we don't,' I say, hoping he can't hear my heart banging through my open mouth.

'You're right.'

'But we don't have to kiss just because everyone thinks we should.'

Why am I talking Charlie out of kissing me?

'Gwynnie?'

'Yeah?'

'Come here.'

I feel his hands reaching out for mine. He takes my hands and pulls me closer to him. The trouble is, neither of us can see where our lips are, so the first thing that happens is that I lick his shoulder.

I am mortified, but Charlie laughs and I suppose it is quite funny, so I laugh too.

'Gwynnie?'

'Yeah?'

'So that we avoid headbutting each other unconscious, how about I hold your face in my hands?'

'Swrmph flllrrr.' I can't speak I'm so excited.

'What was that?'

'I said, *Sure, good idea.*'

He laughs again and lifts his hands to touch

my face and he kind of brushes my boob as he passes. I don't think he meant to . . . but still. He holds my head and pulls me towards him.

Just as we're about to kiss my phone beeps.

'What was that?' he asks.

'I didn't hear anything,' I say.

'I think it was your phone. You better check.'

I hate this flipping phone (ironically enough, it is a flip phone). 'OK,' I say. 'It'll probably be nothing though.'

I flip open the flipping phone. 'It's Paul.'

hi g. im outside. julie innis wont let me in and jennys not answering my txts. come outside and get me will u?

I'm ashamed to say that if Charlie wasn't reading the message over my shoulder I don't know what I would have done.

'We better go and get him,' I say, knowing that Charlie would want me to.

We come out of the cupboard and everyone is looking at us because we've been in there less than two minutes. Paul owes me big time.

I'm too sad to say anything but Charlie says, 'We've decided to boycott this party because our best friends aren't allowed in. Jenny, are you coming?'

Jenny is spinning the bottle.

'Jenny?' I ask.

She waits as it spins.

'Jenny,' says Charlie, 'Paul's waiting outside.'

The bottle lands on Jared Ream, who is the greasiest boy in the whole school. Jenny looks horrified. She stands up and says, 'Yeah, this game is so immature. We're leaving.'

We leave the room looking high and mighty. Which I hope disguises how completely gutted I am.

When we get outside Paul is there and he doesn't look happy.

'Why didn't you answer my texts?' he says to Jenny.

'Did you send me a text, doll?' she replies, all innocent. 'My cell must have been out of batteries.'

I'm not buying that, and Paul's not either. 'Your phone has been out of batteries a lot recently,' he says. 'Every time I text you, you say it's out of batteries. But when I call, it rings.'

Jenny looks like she's just been outsmarted by Einstein.

'Er, well.' She tries a tactic that I must remember for whenever I get a boyfriend (no jokes, please!). She steps towards him, looks him in the eye, then pouts and looks really sad. 'I missed you so much in that party, babe. I wished you were there, but Julie Innis was being such a hag. I thought if I could appeal to her better nature then she would let you in.' Hang on, is that a tear in her eye? I don't like the fact that she is lying to Paul, but there's no denying she's good at it. She continues, 'It turns out that Julie Innis doesn't have a better nature. So that's when I said I wasn't spinning the bottle any more, and I got Gwynnie and Charlie and told them that we had to leave. For you.'

Now that has really got me narked. She basically had to be dragged out of that party by me and Charlie and now she's taking all the credit.

'You were playing spin the bottle?!' Paul is angry.

'No,' says Jenny.

Now, technically, that's true. We were playing Postman's Knock, which is slightly different because the kissing goes on behind closed doors, but that probably makes it worse.

Paul turns to me. 'Is that what happened, Gwynnie?'

Paul used to be my best mate, but Jenny is my new best mate and I don't want her to get in trouble. This is very tricky. Jenny is looking at me like nothing is wrong, like she's a completely devoted girlfriend who made her friends leave the best party ever so that she could be with her boyfriend. She is so sincere that it makes me question my sanity.

'I . . . er . . . I . . .' Suddenly I've become about as coherent as my dad at the Mohans' New Year's Eve party. 'Yeah,' I say. What else can I do?

'Really?' Paul asks.

'Why don't you believe her?' Jenny says, like she's the one with a right to be mad. 'That's what she said, isn't it?'

They're looking at me again, but luckily Charlie comes to my rescue. 'Look, guys, we don't want to get involved. I'll walk Gwynnie home and we'll leave you two to it.'

Charlie Notts is my complete hero. *And* he's said he'll walk me home, which is so nice of him because it is totally out of his way. We leave and Jenny is looking back at us like she wishes she was walking with us. Paul just looks angry. I can hear him saying, 'I'm getting pretty sick of this. First you insist that I meet you at the party rather than at your house because it's more romantic—'

'Well, maybe if you were a bit more romantic I wouldn't have to come up with ways to make you more romantic . . .'

Their argument drifts away like police sirens as me and Charlie head off. 'I hope those two will be all right,' I say. 'They're such a good couple.' It's only after I say it out loud that I realize it's not true. Jenny and Paul have nothing in common and I don't know how they have lasted this long. It's probably something to do with Jenny's big boobs and Paul's ability to look like he's listening when he's not.

'Couples always break up eventually,' says Charlie.

I suppose he's right. The likelihood is that Paul and Jenny won't get married. It's weird – I hated it when Paul and Jenny got together, but now that they might be breaking up it feels wrong.

However, right now I have a new problem and I'm panicking again. I am alone with Charlie. It'll take about ten minutes for us to walk back to my house, and there is no way that I can be interesting for ten minutes. I can't think of a thing to say.

I scan my mind. Why is it only filled with rubbish? There must be something good or funny or insightful I can come up with.

We get all the way to my house without either of us saying a word.

We stand outside my front door. 'Do you know what I like about you, Gwynnie?'

That I'm an idiot? A nutbag? I have stupid skinny legs that make it look like I'm a walking pair of compasses?

'You don't feel the need to talk every second of every day. Some girls just talk and talk and talk and talk, and most of what they say is crap.'

Am I supposed to answer that, or would that make what he just said untrue? I say, 'Thanks,' and leave it at that.

'Is this your house?'

For the first time ever I feel really embarrassed about my house. It's a tiny terraced thing that is in desperate need of a coat of paint. The metre square of lawn in front hasn't been mowed in like a million years and there's a pile of junk that my dad is collecting to make some kind of sculpture. He calls it *art trouvé*. But there is nothing trouvé about it. Whatever trouvé means.

'Would you believe me if I said that I was just looking after it for a friend?'

Charlie laughs. 'Not really. There's a sticker on the window that says, *Spurs Supporter Lives Here*, and I know that you and I are the only people in Northampton stupid enough to support Spurs.'

Suddenly I get a burst of courage and I have no idea where it came from. I lean towards him. I close my eyes and lean and lean and lean. My lips are out and puckered and they aim for him like an arrow in slow motion.

Why haven't I got to his mouth yet? I open my eyes and Charlie's looking at me like I've got a mental disorder. He's bent back, almost at a ninety-degree angle.

His gorgeous face looks confused. 'Are you OK?' he asks. Charlie Notts is so caring.

'I'm fine,' I say. He's not getting it. 'I'm a bit cold.' Perhaps he'll put his arms around me to warm me up.

'You can borrow my coat.' He quickly takes off his coat and hands it to me. 'Give it back on Monday . . . or whenever.'

I take his coat and put it on. Now I'm boiling and I'm sweating up the inside of Charlie's coat. Yuck. *And* he hasn't put his arm around me.

I have another idea. 'I have an itch on my back. On my left shoulder blade. Will you scratch it for me, please?'

He waits for me to turn around, but I don't, so he has to reach his arm around me and scratch my shoulder. He has his arm around me now and it's the most romantic thing since the invention of candlelight. He's leaning forward, and I know what that means. The BB Club told me. He opens his mouth and I know what that means too. I have to remember everything the girls taught me: close my eyes, allow his lips to go round my lips – or is it my lips around his? No pogoing, no washing machines . . . God, I hope I don't get this wrong!

I go in and kiss him. Full on the lips.

'Gwy—' As our lips touch I muffle something that he was trying to say. Maybe he wasn't trying to kiss me after all. But it doesn't matter now. We're actually snogging!

And it's the best thing ever.

chapter 20

I arrive late to the next day's Prom Planning
Committee meeting. This way I know all the
girls will already be there when I walk in. I say,
'Guess what!' like it's nothing and no big deal,
but the fact that I have said *Guess what,* in this loud
announcey-type way means that it obviously is a
big deal.

They all kind of shrug like they are not that
interested.

They will be.

'I'm Charlie Notts girlfriend!!!'

Silence. Not the overjoyed whoops of non-
jealous delight that I was hoping for. I stand there
like a magician who's just done a *ta-da!* But the
rabbit is still in the hat and hasn't disappeared at
all.

'What are you talking about, Gwynnie?' asks
Jenny.

'Oh my God, it's the best thing ever! Me and Charlie are a proper couple!'

'What?' Kimba doesn't sound so sure. 'Charlie Notts? And *you*?'

'Yes.' I don't like the way she said that, like I'm a mental patient and she's one of the doctors in the white coats. But I know that Charlie and me are together now. I am sure of it. A little bit.

'He walked me home and totally snogged me and it was amazing!'

Still silence. Finally Melissa says, 'Look, Gwynnie, I'm not being funny, but you've never snogged anyone before—'

'Jenny!' I squeal. 'You said you wouldn't tell.'

'This is the BB Club, Gwynnie. Telling them is not telling.'

Somehow I'm not sure if that's true, but it doesn't matter any more so I let it slide.

Melissa continues. 'Maybe you thought you snogged him but you didn't.'

'Of course I did! We were outside my door. And then he kissed me.' Technically I kissed him, but what's the difference? We kissed.

'Did you use tongues or was it just a peck on the cheek?' asks Jenny.

'Definite tongues. First we staircased, then we pogoed for a——'

'TMI, Gwynnie,' interrupts Melissa with a hand raised.

'Thanks very much,' I reply.

'That means *too much information*.'

'Oh.' I'm still learning. 'Still,' I continue, 'we kissed for ages. Like about two minutes.'

'That's a shame,' says Jenny. 'Oh well, maybe he had to get home.'

'Is that not very long?' She's instantly made me feel bad. 'He did say that he had to go home.'

'Ooooh.' They all do this noise at the same time. The way they do it makes it sound like a bad thing.

I defend myself. 'But you said that maybe he had to go home.'

'Yeah, but if he *said* he had to go home it sounds like he was making excuses to go, rather than having to go. Do you see the difference?'

I totally do! Oh this is awful. Charlie Notts kissed me and then couldn't get away fast enough. 'Do you think I've blown it?'

Elizabeth goes all reassuring. 'No, no. It doesn't definitely mean that. So when did he ask you out?'

'What do you mean?'

'How did he say it? Was he like, *Will you go out with me?*' Elizabeth looks all dreamy and smiley as if she's imagining some romantic movie. 'Or, *Will you be my girlfriend?* or, *Can I be your boyfriend?*'

'He didn't say any of those things.'

Elizabeth's face falls a little but then she smiles at me again. The smile is not as strong as it was before.

'But we kissed for ages so that must mean I'm his girlfriend.'

'Oh, Gwynnie,' Kimba says, shaking her head, 'you really don't know anything, do you?'

I would shout at her that *she's* the one who doesn't know anything, but when I look around they are all shaking their heads in the same way.

Jenny says, 'You're not going out with a boy until he asks you out formally or refers to you as his girlfriend.'

'But—'

'No buts, sweetie. Those are the rules. Or else how do you know if it was just a snog for the sake of a snog, or you are proper boyfriend and girlfriend?'

I think back to what happened and wonder

how I could be so stupid. He tried to snog me in the cupboard but that's because it was Postman's Knock. *I* was the one who snogged him outside my house. He played along with it for the shortest time possible, out of pity. Then he said he had to go home. Obviously to get out of it.

'Oh, sweetie, don't be upset.' Jenny is so nice sometimes. 'At least you got your first snog.'

'I suppose.' Jenny's right. At least someone found me not too hideous to give me a pity snog. But this is not how I thought today would go. When I woke up this morning I thought I had a boyfriend, and that he was the most gorgeous boy in the whole school. But an hour later, it turns out that I'm a delusional nutbag. I tell the BB girls that I've just remembered I have to leave.

'But we're planning prom!' says Elizabeth. 'We're on to decorations, and how we're going to have our hair.'

'Balloons, streamers and a disco mirror ball,' I say. This is from a movie that my mum used to like.

They all make impressed *Ahhh* noises about the mirror ball.

'And I was hoping that I could borrow your

ghd's, Jenny, so that I could have my hair super-straight.'

'Sorry, Gwynnie. I can't lend out my ghd's to bronze members.'

'What? Why?'

'It's part of the bronze membership deal; ghd's count as a privilege.'

I'm not sure if this is fair. 'Are you doing everyone else's hair?'

'Yes.'

'Even Elizabeth and Tanya?'

'They are full members.'

'But they haven't got their belly-buttons pierced.'

'Elizabeth and Tanya are founding members so the policy is different.

'I don't know, Jenny,' says Elizabeth. 'Couldn't we just—'

'Be quiet, Elizabeth,' says Jenny. 'You're still only a silver member.'

I look around at the others but they've all started messing with their phones or rummaging in their bags. Only Elizabeth looks up for a second to mouth, *Sorry*.

'But if I get my belly-button pierced my dad will kill me and then I won't be able to go to prom anyway.' I try to get off on compassionate grounds.

'You have to get your priorities straight,' says Kimba. I knew she was behind all this bronze privilege stuff. 'If you really want to be in this club you could get your belly-button pierced, then hide it from your dad until after prom.'

I can't take this. In the last five minutes I've lost my boyfriend and been told I'll either have rubbish hair for prom or get stabbed in the stomach. 'I've really got to go,' I say, and leg it out of there.

*

I'm already on the street when Paul calls me. I don't really want to talk to anyone. But Paul's not really anyone.

'Hi, Gwyndle.'

I've only just remembered that I forgot to ask Jenny what happened with her and Paul because I was too busy obsessing over the shortest non-relationship since the Big Bang. Maybe that's why she was so mean to me just now.

'Hey, Paul. How are you?'

'I'm OK. A bit bored really.'

'Are you not seeing Jenny later?'

'I dunno. We sort of had that thing last night—'

'You didn't break up, did you?' For some reason I don't think I could take it if they broke up.

'No.'

I breathe a sigh of relief. 'That's good then. I mean, loads of couples have arguments and it all works out fine.' I don't know who I am trying to convince here, him or me.

'Yeah, she says she just needs some space to think.'

In the old days I would have said that I didn't know that Jenny knew how to think, but I let it drop. 'Well, that's cool then.'

'Yeah. Except I didn't know that Jenny knew how to think.' He laughs, and I do too. 'Sorry, I know she's your friend now.'

'That's OK. We're allowed to make jokes at our friends' expense. Just as long as they don't find out.' I wink down the phone at him, before I remember that he can't see me.

Then Paul says, 'Do you think Spurs will win the final?'

I don't even have to think. I know. 'They'll do really well in the first half and then mess it up in the second.'

'You never know.'

'We haven't won the FA Cup since, like, a million years before the dinosaurs were born.' I'm saying all this stuff and realizing that all the things I thought I didn't care about any more, I totally do care about. 'It would be so great to see Spurs lift the cup.'

'Don't hold your breath, Gwynnie.'

'It's all about who turns up on the day, Paul.'

'It's a game of two halves, Gwynnie.'

'All we need is one more goal than the other guys, Paul.'

We're laughing, and it feels like old times again. I'm properly back in a good mood, and I thought I'd never be in a good mood ever after realizing that I was wrong about me and Charlie.

'So where you going to watch it?' he asks the question I hoped he wasn't going to ask. 'Are you and your dad doing your normal tradition of the Old Pack Horse?'

Me and my dad have watched the FA Cup final at my dad's local pub every year of my life. They now reserve a table for us, even though everyone wants a table because it's FA

Cup final day. 'The thing is,' I tell Paul, 'this year I won't be able to because I'm helping with prom.'

'Oh. Right. Have you told your dad this?' Paul is acting like I'm letting *him* down rather than my dad.

'Not yet. But it's not like he won't be able to find anyone to watch it with.'

'Yeah, but you better tell him quick in case he has made special plans or something.'

Why is Paul being so weird? 'Well, Mr Agony Aunt, I would speak to him, but he's always out these days.'

'I know. He's always over here.'

'What's he doing round there?'

'Helping my mum in the garden.' Paul is sounding more and more shifty by the second.

'Why is my dad always round with your mum? Do you think there's something going on between those two?'

'No,' he says, all defensively. 'But would it be so bad if there was? Your dad is a nice guy, nicer than my dad ever was. He might be good for her.'

I think about this for a minute. I suppose Paul is right. Angela is great, and my dad is pretty great too – for a gormless fool – but the feeling I get when I think of them together is like the feeling I get when I think of Paul and Jenny breaking up. I don't want it to happen, but I'm not sure why.

chapter 21

'Gwynnie, you will look brilliant if you do this,' says Elizabeth, beaming at me. 'And the BB Club will have to make you a gold member.'

Which means I can use the ghd's for prom.

So here we are, in some dodgy tattoo parlour in town, about to get my belly-button pierced. I asked Elizabeth to come with me for support. Normally I would have asked Jenny, but she hasn't been answering her phone recently. And anyway, I know Elizabeth will be nicer about it if I scream like a girl. I feel like she's standing over my death bed.

'Where do you want it, luv?' asks the piercing lady.

I'm a bit worried because I've told her twice that I want my belly-button pierced, I am lying on this table, and I've pulled up my top so my belly-button is exposed. Where does she think I want it?

Elizabeth answers for me. 'In her navel.'

Where the hell is my navel? It sounds like it's somewhere at sea. 'No, I don't!' I quickly shout. 'I want it in my belly-button.'

Elizabeth whispers to me. 'Your navel *is* your belly-button!'

'Oh,' I say. 'I thought you said eyebrow.'

The woman who is about to make a hole in my body sort of nods as she says, 'Right, OK,' except I can't properly understand her as she has her tongue pierced and her lip pierced. She's wearing all black and her hair is dyed bright orange, which makes her look like a battery. She has tattoos all over her, ones that say *Mum*, ones that say *Dad* . . . She has fairies and angels, all with gigantic boobs that are out there for the world to see. She has five piercings in each ear, one in her eyebrow, and even a few in her arm that stretch her skin in a nasty way. But if she has gone through it this many times, it must mean it's not painful.

She looks around for something and then asks, 'Have either of you got a pen?' Elizabeth quickly gives her a Zac Efron biro from her bag. I wonder if she is going to make me sign something, but she makes a mark on my stomach, just below the belly-button. 'Is that about right, luv?'

I nod. For some reason I thought they would do all this with lasers and precision tools and medical experts. I had no idea that Zac Efron would be involved.

'Don't worry, Gwynnie,' says Elizabeth. 'I'm sure it won't hurt that much.'

The Battery nods in agreement and pulls out this humongous needle gun that looks like the kind of thing they tranquillize rhinos with. 'Besides,' the Battery says, 'some people like the pain.'

'OK,' I say, like a soldier about to go into battle. 'I'm ready.'

She puts the needle-gun thing on my stomach. Elizabeth holds my hand and pulls this face like she thinks it will definitely hurt. But Elizabeth has not put holes in *her* stomach, so what does Elizabeth know?

The Battery pulls the trigger and there's a sort of *click-thud* noise. It turns out that Elizabeth knows everything.

'Ow ow ow ow ow ow ow!' I am in more pain that I have ever been in in my life. More pain than when David Kaddimacaza slide-tackled me and took off my little toenail. More pain than when Jenny persuaded me that waxing my armpit was a good idea. I'm sure being shot with a real gun could not be this bad.

Elizabeth is screaming in agony too and I'm touched that some sort of psychic connection has given my friend sympathy pains. 'Gwynnie!' she shouts, 'you're breaking my hand!'

Oh.

The skin on my stomach is all red and bleeding, but there is a metallic ring in it, and that's all that matters. Elizabeth starts swaying a little bit, and the music in the background changes to a low sort of hum.

'There you go sweetheart,' says the Battery. 'That'll be twenty quid.'

I look at her. And then I throw up on the floor.

'That's going to cost you extra.'

*

Elizabeth puts a cold flannel to my head. 'You can lie down if you want,' she says.

'I'm fine,' I say.

'You don't look fine.' Elizabeth is wincing. 'You look . . . green.'

We're in her bedroom and I sit forward in the

chair to look at myself in the mirror on her dresser. Just the movement of leaning forward makes me feel even more sick and I groan. Then I see my reflection and I groan even louder.

'This can't be normal,' I say. I'm definitely a pinkish shade of green. Like cheap toilet paper. Or a lettuce gone off. I hoist myself up and over to the bed.

'Have you got a bucket?' I ask Elizabeth in a panic.

Elizabeth looks equally panicky. I know her fluffy rug is new after she spilled Ribena over her carpet and she had to cover it up so her mum wouldn't see the stain. The rug looks like Macaroni, only bright blue. 'Are you going to be sick?'

'No,' I reply, 'I want to put it over my head!'

Elizabeth laughs. She has this really funny laugh that I have never properly heard before – it sounds like a pig with the giggles when it's got a cold. Her laugh makes me laugh, and that helps to make me not want to vom all over her fluffy rug. She slaps her hands over her face. 'Sorry.'

'For what?'

'Jenny says I sound really ugly when I laugh and I shouldn't inflict it on people.'

I frown at her and sit up a little. 'Your laugh is hilarious!' I tell her.

'But I don't want to be hilarious,' she says, and she looks a bit sad. 'Jenny has this pretty little laugh that makes her sound like a small child who knows a rude secret. All the boys love it.'

'Jenny could make ballet lessons compulsory and all the boys would love it,' I reply.

'I know!' Elizabeth says. A tear rolls down her cheek. 'How does she do it? Why do they all like her so much?'

I'm a bit shocked. She must be sad that even a muppet like me has managed to snog someone and she hasn't snogged anyone yet. I didn't realize that Elizabeth was so unhappy; she is always so sweet to everyone and nice to be around. 'I don't know,' I say. 'But it might be something to do with the three chicken fillets she stuffs down her bra.'

Elizabeth looks at me through wide, wet eyes. 'She uses *three* chicken fillets?!'

I nod. 'Four, on special occasions.'

'I knew there was something different about her!' Elizabeth shakes her head in surprise. But then her face falls. 'It will take more than chicken fillets to get someone to snog me.'

Crying's not my speciality. I haven't done it in ages and I'm not really sure how to handle it in other people. When I used to cry my dad and Kevin would tell me jokes until I started laughing. Or sometimes they would just let me cry and they'd leave the room. I realize that might not cut it in this situation.

What was it my mum used to do?

'Come here,' I order her. Elizabeth looks at me. I open my arms all big, just like my mum did, and give her a hug.

Oh God, it hasn't worked. I've made it worse — she's crying even harder now! 'Sorry, Elizabeth,' I say, and pull away.

Elizabeth seems a little embarrassed but she smiles at me. A tear drops from her cheek and lands on the rug.

I'll try my dad's tactic. 'Hey, where's your dog?'

'Macaroni?' She looks confused like she has no idea why I've brought up Macaroni at a time like this.

'Yeah.' I eye her suspiciously.

'I don't know. My mum might have taken him for a walk. Why?'

'I haven't seen that dog since you got this rug . . . Coincidence? I don't think so.'

She laughs and coughs at the same time.

'I'm not making any accusations, but if I find a bottle of blue dye anywhere I'm calling the RSPCA.'

The piglet laugh is back.

'And if I find out that you used to have a dog called Cheese, you are in really deep trouble!'

Elizabeth now sounds like a pig with not just a cold, but with swine flu. 'You're so funny, Gwynnie!' She pauses for a sec. 'That's why all the boys like you.'

All the boys like *me*? This is news.

'How do you get the boys to like you?'

'Elizabeth, you're asking a bald man for hairstyling tips.'

She glances at the floor before looking up again, like she's gearing up to say something huge. 'But Paul likes you,' she says.

'Yeah, but I've known Paul my whole——'

'And Ranjit.' Suddenly she goes bright red and can't look at me.

'Yeah, but Ranjit and——' Hang on a minute . . . 'Elizabeth, do you like Ranj?'

She shakes her head a little too quickly. 'No,' she says.

I don't say anything; I've heard that's a good way to get a confession.

'No!' she says again. Then once she catches on to my sneaky smile she says, 'Ranjit would never feel the same way anyway. He doesn't like girls like me.' She gets up and walks over to fiddle with something on top of her cupboard, like that's the end of the conversation.

But I'm not letting it rest like that. 'I have no idea what kind of girls Ranjit likes,' I tell her. 'But I can tell you what he *does* like.' She flicks her head round really quickly. 'I mean, if you want to know . . .'

She grins at me cos she knows I'm teasing.

'He supports Aston Villa, so that means he's a glutton for punishment. Um, his favourite food is fizzy cola bottles.'

Elizabeth is nodding along, as if she's memorizing all this for a gameshow.

'His favourite film is *The Sixth Sense*.'

'I've seen that!' she says, all excited. 'It's a great film!'

'Yeah, but he's seen it twelve times, which I think is a bit weird, but there you go.'

She looks thoughtful.

'He's pretty cool really, Elizabeth,' I say to her. 'You should go for it.'

She's still thinking.

'Come on, if an idiot like me can snog Charlie Notts, then there's no reason that a cool chick like you couldn't get Ranjit Mohan.'

'But . . .' she pauses again, 'what will Jenny and the others say if I go out with him? Will they laugh at me?'

'Who cares what they think?' I say.

'Thanks, Gwynnie.' She smiles at me and then pulls me in for another big hug. 'Oh, sorry,' she says and pulls back. 'Are you feeling OK now?'

And I realize that I'm feeling fine.

chapter 22

I stagger into my house, feeling better after eight of Elizabeth's mum's homemade cookies. I go into the kitchen to see if my dad notices my cool new piercing – he never notices anything.

'Hi, Dad,' I say, all bright and breezy as if everything is normal.

He doesn't even look up from the sports pages, so everything is certainly normal there.

'Have we got any muesli, Dad?'

I knew that would get his attention. He's always banging on about me eating nothing but chips and bread and saying one day I'll be as fat as a beach ball and I always say, *Chance would be a fine thing*. At least if I was a beach ball then maybe I might get to go to the beach.

He looks at me like I've gone crazy. Then he looks me up and down. Then he notices my belly-button ring. Then he's the one who goes crazy.

'What on earth have you done to yourself?!' he shouts.

Why does my dad have to notice everything?

'What?' I say, like I don't know what he's talking about. Like it's none of his business. Which it totally isn't.

'Don't pretend you don't know what I'm talking about. What is that thing in your stomach?'

'Oh, don't worry, Dad, that's just a piercing.'

'How could you?!' he shouts. 'When did you do that?'

I'm tempted to say, *Years ago*, but he actually looks angry, so I just go with the truth. 'This morning. At this properly professional place run by a woman that really knew her stuff.' I didn't say I would tell the whole truth.

'Don't you have to be sixteen to get yourself pierced?'

'She thought I was sixteen.'

'Is that because you told her you were sixteen?' he asks.

'Well . . .' That might also be true.

'Gwynnie, the reason you have to be sixteen is because you have to be old enough to make considered choices. I mean, even if you take that out now—'

'I'm not taking it out!' That would be a total waste of forty pounds.

'What I'm saying is, even if you take it out, you will still have a scar on your skin for the rest of your life.'

'I know that. I'm not a child!'

'Yes, you *are* a child.'

I'm so insulted.

'What I mean is, you are not an adult and you have no idea about the consequences of your actions.'

Why do parents always do all this *consequences of your actions* stuff? 'Why don't you just leave me alone? I don't bother you about your life. Not that it's much of a life, working at a sports shop and flirting with Angela Shields!' OK, that was a bit harsh, and I feel bad for saying it as soon as I say it.

'What's wrong with you these days, Gwynnie? We used to be friends, but recently you're . . .'

'I'm what?'

Dad thinks about what to say for a second before quietly uttering, '. . . a little unpleasant.'

That is the rudest thing that anyone has ever said to me! Coming from my own father means that it's twenty billion times worse. 'Well, you're

. . . you're . . . you're the gingerest person in the world!' I don't know if that hurt or not. 'I'm going to my room. And as I'm so *unpleasant* you'll be happy to stay away from me.' That's more like it. I slam the kitchen door and storm upstairs.

chapter 23

I want everyone to see my new piercing. On Monday I walk to school in a top that's so small it's not much more than a bra, and tracksuit bottoms that I push down low so I'm showing off as much of my stomach as possible. The whole school is in assembly and I think they are all talking about me. For once, that feels pretty good.

Then The Dazzler says, 'Gwendolyn, please would you stand up?'

A few months ago this would have been like I was man of the match in my worst nightmare. But right now I'm OK with it. I stand up.

'Everyone look at Gwendolyn Lewis.'

Everyone looks at me and I feel like a bit of a celeb.

'This is a perfect example of what I was talking about at the beginning of term. We can not have students dressing like this and continue to maintain an image of decency. As I mentioned weeks ago, there is a new school uniform in place . . .'

I think I know what's coming.

'You have had plenty of time to purchase one. As of tomorrow, anyone not in the correct attire will spend two weeks in detention.'

Two weeks in detention would probably be worth it.

'*And* the offender will not be allowed to go to the prom on Saturday.'

The assembly hall completely erupts. I have never heard anything like it. Take That or Madonna playing at Wembley would have made less noise. Michael Jackson coming back from the dead would have barely registered compared to this. The end of the world would have been a quiet day in the Lake District when put against the wailing and gnashing of teeth coming from Northampton Hill High.

'You have driven me to this and it's your fault.'

He means you, like, you the whole school, but it sounds like you, Gwendolyn Lewis.

Every other word I hear is my name. Just as

I'm thinking there is no way that this could be worse, Mr Roberts tops it. Above the din I can just hear him saying, '. . . regulation . . . blazer . . . tie . . .' and the word I was dreading above all: '. . . skirt.'

My knees begin to buckle. I sit down quickly without waiting for permission and feel like turning into one of those proper nutters that live in a padded cell and rock back and forth.

As we file out of assembly I can hear Kimba say to Tanya, 'I told Gwynnie that top was too much. Now we have to wear uniform . . . all because of her.'

Which is a complete lie, but I hate myself so much right now that it's almost nice to have someone else hate me too — it makes me feel included.

*

It's the next morning, and no matter how many pictures of Outer Mongolia I show my dad, I can not get him to agree to move there. I am going to live and die in England. Possibly in a few hours, when I get to school and they all decide to kill me.

I get dressed in my room and leave the skirt till last. I do all my make-up and curl my hair with the straighteners (which should be impossible, by definition). This is avoidance of the inevitable. Finally I put on the skirt and look in the mirror.

It's a plain black A-line skirt that stops at my knees. Then there are my knees: they're stupidly knobbly, like a bag of marbles, and they are covered with scars where I picked off old football scabs, and scabs on scabs on scars on scabs. I bought some tights after school yesterday so no one will see, but there is no hiding my skinny legs. It would be OK if I could wear leggings, but someone asked the Dazzler yesterday and he said, 'Under no circumstances.' I wonder if that includes me?

I wait outside Jenny's house so that we can walk in together and not feel so terrible. It's only OK to look like a fool if you're with someone else who looks the same. She is still in her *I'm not answering my phone* phase so she looks pretty surprised to see me standing outside her door. Somehow she has managed to look really good in her uniform. Not cool exactly — no one could look cool in school uniform — but she has fashioned it up with these funky tights, and a way of tying the tie so it looks short and fat. Mine looks like I have a piece of string dangling round my neck.

I'm speechless for a minute before I ask, 'How did you get your skirt so short?' They are supposed to be regulation length.

She lifts up her fitted shirt and shows me that she has rolled the skirt over itself at the waist to make it shorter. 'Easy, see. Anyone could do it.'

'Not me,' I say. 'I have to find a way of hiding my skinny legs. They are hideous.'

'Yeah, you're right,' she says. 'Never mind. Maybe you could get a longer skirt and call it a maxi dress.'

I pretend to know what a maxi dress is and nod along.

She's pretty quiet on the way there and I think she must be dreading our first uniform day as much as I am. I take a deep breath as we approach the school gates.

'We'll have to stick close together.' I try to hook her arm with mine but she pulls away.

'It's OK, thanks.'

'What's up?' I ask her. Jenny seems angry with me.

'Nothing. Oh look, there's the rest of the girls!' And with that she darts off towards the BB gang, leaving me alone.

In the playground there's this weird thing in the air because we're all wearing uniform for the first time. Everyone is speaking to everyone else, telling their story about how they hate how we look and how their parents are writing letters to the school board to get it changed back to how it was. But they are kind of enjoying themselves too. It's something to bond over.

I walk in and Northampton Hill High goes quiet. Apparently the school hasn't completely forgiven me for being the cause of all this. They look at me and shake their heads.

'Thanks a lot, Gwendolyn Lewis!'

Great, a Year 11 knows my name but only to shout abuse at me.

I hurry over to my friends in the BB Club. (There's no point having your belly-button pierced when it's hidden under a shirt.) If I thought we all looked the same before, we *definitely* all look the same now: navy-blue blazers with a badge, and skirts to match. But all the other girls have short skirts that show off their nice legs. Even Tanya has rolled up her skirt because her mum is not around to stop her.

I try to say, 'Hi,' like everything is fine when it's completely not.

'Hi, Gwynnie,' says Elizabeth. 'What do we all look like, eh?'

The rest of them all nod hello to me, then sort of turn away a little. Jenny stands a few metres from me. They're so far away I feel short-sighted.

'I've never seen you in a skirt before, Gwynnie,' says Tanya, who stops herself from saying I look OK because that would be a downright lie.

Paul and Ranjit come over, talking about who is wearing a clip-on tie and who had to get their mum to tie theirs for them. 'Hey, Gwynnie,' Ranjit says, 'aren't you Miss Popular today?' He laughs. 'I think everyone hates you!' He says it as if he's filling me in on the weather forecast: foggy, with a chance of dislike.

'Really?' I mumble, now terrified.

'Yup,' he says, not realizing that this is worse than that time when Spurs lost to West Ham due to dodgy lasagne. 'I've heard someone's even drawn a tombstone with the words *R.I.P. Gwynnie* on the wall in the girls' toilets.'

'Is that true?'

'Actually,' says Kimba, 'it says *R.I.P. Skinny Gwynnie.*'

'That's not true,' says Paul. 'It's just a rumour.'

This is really bad.

'Don't we all look smart?' Charlie Notts has just joined the group and I feel like hiding behind a bush. 'All I need is a pair of thick-rimmed glasses and a bowl haircut and then I would be the uncoolest person in the world.'

'Second only to Gwynnie,' says Kimba.

Charlie looks at me with pity. 'Yeah. I heard about the tombstone in the toilets, Gee. I'm sorry.'

I have a huge lump in my throat and I want to run away. But the only place to go is the toilets and then I would have to walk past everyone else in the school shouting at me, only to arrive in a room with a picture of my own grave in it. At least my friends will just insult me once and then it'll be over. I hope.

'Gwynnie,' says Kimba, 'we had an emergency meeting about you last night on MSN. We would kind of prefer it if you didn't hang out with us for a while.'

'What? Why?' I ask.

'Well,' she explains, 'everyone kind of despises you, and we don't want them to depise us by association.'

'Jenny?' I plead to my best friend.

Jenny starts rummaging in her bag as if she hasn't heard me. I *was* being a bit of a knob yesterday, showing off my new piercing like that, but I can't believe that the exact thing I thought would make me cool and popular has made me the most uncool and unpopular person in the history of high school.

'Sorry, Gwynnie,' Melissa says, 'but we have to think of the reputation of the BB Club.'

I feel sick.

'Yeah,' Kimba says, obviously loving being the bearer of such bad news, 'and we are also dismissing you from the Prom Planning Committee.'

'Hey!' I say, feeling a bit angry. 'I thought you were supposed to be my friends.'

'Perhaps you shouldn't even come to prom at all,' she says, as if she's pointing out something that I should have realized on my own.

'Kimba,' says Elizabeth, her voice shaking a little, 'Gwynnie's right; she's a BB girl and we should stick by her. Everyone will forget about this after a while.'

Kimba shoots Elizabeth a look. 'No one has forgotten about *your* incident, Elizabeth, and that happened in Year 5. Every day for the rest of forever the pupils of Northampton Hill High will get dressed for school and curse Gwynnie's name.'

'Not the rest of forever,' I say. But maybe she's right.

'But still,' continues Elizabeth, 'Gwynnie is—'

'Elizabeth, do you want your membership reduced to bronze too?'

Now Elizabeth is getting flack for sticking up for me. If I don't walk away now I will cry. 'Forget it then!' I shout. 'Some friends you are! I'll see you around,' I say, and I start running. I'm heading for my grave in the girls' toilets. If my dad doesn't let me change school then I am going to Mongolia by myself.

I hear Charlie say, really loudly, 'Don't be rude to Gwynnie, all right?'

And Kimba says, 'What do you care?'

As far away as I am I can still hear his answer. 'Because I want to ask her something, and you can't cuss her like that.'

What does he want to ask me?

'Gwynnie, wait!' He shouts it really, *really* loudly this time so the whole school looks. He runs to catch up with me so I stop and let him. He says, 'Gwynnie, erm . . .'

'Yes, Charlie.' This totally isn't real.

'Will you go to the prom with me?'

I'm too shocked to say anything.

'What do you say, Gwynnie? Will you be my date on Saturday?'

I am looking at him like he just asked me to join Girls Aloud, mouth open, eyes wide – I must look ridiculous. But the whole entire world is watching Charlie Notts ask me to the prom.

'Yes, please,' I squeak. (OK, the *please* was possibly a bit much.)

Me and Charlie are going to the prom together. And if he doesn't ask me out properly, then I'll just have to ask him.

chapter 24

'Hey, Dad, how's it hanging?' I say as my Dad walks into the living room.

'It's hanging superbly, Gwyndoe, just bloody superbly.' He gives me a big kiss on the top of my head, which I let slide.

'Why are you in such a good mood?' I ask him.

'Wouldn't you like to know?' he says.

I would, but I don't want to give him the satisfaction of asking when he's looking so smug. 'Have you just taken a pill that can make you happy but will make your hair even more frizzy?'

'No, Gwynnie, I haven't. And I wouldn't need one as I am extremely frizzy and as happy as a clam.'

'Tell me.'

'No.'

'Tell me, Dad.'

'No.'

'You know you can't keep a secret.' I roll my eyes in this overly dramatic way. 'Tell me now and then we can skip over the whining and pleading and get on to your boring secret, then have dinner.' I'm not being *unpleasant* here, I am only teasing him and he knows it.

'Oh, Gwynnie . . . This is *so completely* not boring.' Dad thinks he's speaking like me, but I so completely don't speak like that. Oh.

'Tell me or I'll tickle you.' My dad's weakness is tickling. I stand up and get him at the back of the neck, where I know he's most vulnerable. He does that thing that's sort of in between laughing and screaming in agony, and then he yells, 'Stop! I surrender! I'll tell you everything.'

'You'd be rubbish in a torture situation, Dad. They wouldn't need a dripping tap, just a feather duster.'

Dad looks at me and he's smiling. I can see that he's really properly smiling like I haven't seen him smile in ages. Not since Mum was alive and he had his proper job at the warehouse and Mum had her part-time work at Dixons and we didn't have a lot of money but we were fine.

Suddenly Dad goes all serious.

'Gwynnie, I'm sorry if I've been a bit of a rubbish dad sometimes.'

I don't say anything. I could tell him he's not a rubbish dad, because he's not. Well, not all of the time. But I'm waiting to see what bombshell he's about to drop.

'Since your mother died I've found it really difficult to manage on my own . . . with everything . . . There's a lot of stuff that I feel I have messed up that I know your mother would have handled better, and there is a lot stuff you have missed out on.'

'I don't need stuff, Dad.' When have I ever needed stuff?

He takes a breath and then continues. 'Angela wanted me to tell you that you can always come to her if you ever need any – erm – *girl talk*—' Oh no, he's not going to talk about condoms and diseases again, is he? 'And she knows that she's not your mum and she'd never be as good as your mum, but . . .'

What's Angela got to do with anything? Please don't tell me he's marrying Angela.

'Is this about Angela?' There's this weird crack in my voice and I realize that I am on the verge of crying. It sometimes happens when people start talking about Mum in a serious way.

'This isn't about Angela at all really, and I don't know why I brought it up. I just wanted to say that I know things have been difficult since Mum died . . . And I'm sorry that I ruined your birthday by not having any money. If there was anything I could change about the past couple of months, that would be it.'

'It's OK, Dad.' And it was OK. So why did I make such a big deal about it at the time?

'Anyway, I wanted to make it up to you by doing something brilliant. Just the two of us.'

'You don't have to, Dad.' Part of me is excited that maybe he's got us tickets to New York Fashion Week, but part of me is worried that he is about to suggest counting sparrows at Bradlaugh Fields.

'So . . .'

'Yes?'

'You know how Spurs have kicked the bums of every other team in the FA Cup for the first time since 1991?'

'Yeah.' Doesn't everyone know that?

'And you know that we usually watch the final down the pub with the lads?'

'Yeah.' I can see where he is going with this but I don't dare to dream it's true.

'Gwynnie . . .' He makes it all dramatic like he's a gameshow host. 'I've . . . gotusticketstotheFACupfinal!!!'

This is amazing! So amazing that I can't register what he's saying. My mouth hangs open like a goal when the keeper's been sent off, while my dad does this dance that makes him look like he's stirring three different pans of soup at the same time, two with his hands and one with his bottom. 'We're going to see Spurs?' I ask. I've only ever seen them play four times.

'Yup.'

'In the FA Cup final?' I will probably never see Spurs in the FA Cup final again.

'Yup.'

'This is the best thing you have ever done for me ever!' I run over and gave him a big hug.

'I thought we'd make a day of it; go down to London, watch Tottenham lift the FA Cup, and then after we've shouted ourselves hoarse, get something to eat somewhere, like pizza or something, before we come home.'

I can picture it now: there we are with

thousands of screaming Spurs fans. It's the eighty-ninth minute, it's two all, and Andros Townsend makes the most amazing tackle before passing it down the line to Frazier Campbell who lobs it over to Robbie Keane who takes it round one of their defenders, then two, then three, before chipping it over the keeper and scoring the most amazing goal since Gazza's 1991 stonker against Arsenal. The crowd will jump up in amazement and when the ball finally passes the goal line everyone will go mental and start hugging and bawling. Then the ref will blow for full time and everyone will go even more mental because they will realize that we have actually done it. Then Charlie Notts will ring me and ask if I saw it, and I'll be like, *Saw it? I'm here!* Then he'll tell me that I am the most amazing girl he has ever met and he'll say he wants more than anything to be my boyfriend.

'Thank you so much, Dad. You're the best.'

'Well,' he says, like it's no big deal or anything, 'I figured that we were doing nothing special on Saturday so . . .' He trails off when he sees my face.

Nothing special.

'What's the matter?'

'Nothing, Dad. This is brilliant.' But absolutely everything is the matter.

'I am the happiest man in the whole entire world,' he says. 'I am going with my favourite daughter to watch my favourite team play. You can't get better than that . . .'

The FA Cup final is the same day as prom. What the flan am I going to do?

chapter 25

Hi c soz but i can't come to prom on sat ☹

I'm texting Charlie. If I told him I was going to the FA Cup final he might understand. But I can't tell him I'm still into football or else he'll transfer my number back into his Mates list, and I'll never be his girlfriend no matter how many eyelashes I pull out or chicken fillets I put in. Instead I tell him it's something I can't get out of.

u c the thing is is that my 2nd cousin twice removed is getting married and the wedding is in scotland and its on sat which is the same day as prom and i really have 2 go coz she is like my cousin and gives me the best pressies so it wld b properly rude if i didnt go.

The text is running on into three, but I have to do it in a way that he knows I'd be there if I could.

i mean im fine and everything but my dad wont let
me stay here without him so i really have 2 go 2 it.
im so so soz ☹

Then, I add, for extra good measure,

o and im a bridesmaid as well so I definitely can't
come

That should do it. I wonder if he's going to call back, saying he's going to cry and beg me to go to prom with him. I wait and wait . . . nothing. No reply. Nothing. What do I do now?

I'll call Jenny. She's always brilliant at things like this. I know they suspended me from the BB Club, but Jenny didn't say anything about not being her friend any more.

'Jenny?'

'Sorry, Gwynnie, I can't talk to you right now—'

'But I need your help.'

She must be able to tell that I mean it from the tone of my voice. She makes the time for me. 'What is it?'

'I can't go to prom with Charlie! I can't go to prom at all!'

'Why?'

'My stupid dad isn't letting me.' She doesn't need to know the truth.

'Is this because you got your belly-button pierced?'

'Um, yeah.' Good one. Why didn't I think of that?

'Oh my God, hun. This is the worst thing that could ever happen to you.'

I'm so glad she realized.

'What did Charlie say?' she asks. 'Did he mind?'

'I've texted Charlie and he hasn't texted me back. I don't know whether it's because he's angry or upset or he thinks I hate him . . . Which I don't, obviously.'

Jenny goes quiet. That's so unlike her and I am pleased that she understands how serious this situation is.

Finally she says, 'Or he could have just not got the message yet. You know? Like maybe he's off helping out with some orphans or playing soccer or something.'

It would be so like Charlie to be helping out with orphans.

'But what if he *is* upset? Should I call him?'

'No!' she says quickly, so I know it must be the right answer. 'If he's not upset it will be fully weird if you ring him and ask if he's upset. If he *is* upset then that's good. You're playing hard to get and boys love the chase.'

'Are you sure? Are you sure that I shouldn't just call him and tell him that it's not my fault that I can't go with him.'

'I'll tell you what – I'll give him a call and find out what he's thinking.'

'Thank you so much, Jenny. I don't know what I'd do without a friend like you.' I really don't.

After the phone call I go downstairs to make a really big celebratory bacon sandwich. Everything was looking bad before, and it's still looking bad, but I feel like Jenny is on the case and is going to sort it out like a fairy godmother. But without the grey hair and the mice and the pumpkins.

*

When I get into the kitchen I see a note from Dad saying that he is round at Angela's again. I've had enough of all Dad's sneaking around. I am going to go over to Paul's to see if I can catch them at it.

I'm at Paul and Angela's front door in like thirty milliseconds, all ready to confront and expose them in a big *a-ha!*-type way. I just hope they are not doing it or anything, because then

I would have to sign up for a lobotomy to erase the memory from my mind. Paul answers the door and he looks kind of funny. As if maybe he's seen them doing it and he has already been for the lobotomy.

I have no time for niceties. 'Where's my dad?'

'Not here. They said they were going to the garden centre or something.'

Hmm. 'That's a bit of a couple-y thing to do, don't you think?'

Paul sort of mumbles, 'What would I know about couple-y things?'

'What?'

'Nothing.'

'Oh.' Maybe he's in on it.

'Do you want to come in for a bit?' he asks.

I am pulled out of my daydream by Paul's question as I realize that I've been staring into space like an astronaut. 'Sorry? What?'

'Do you want to go to the park and play footie?'

'Oh, Paul, you're a doll, you really are. You know I don't play soccer any more—'

'I don't get you these days, Gwynnie! You used to be a laugh, and now you just act like an idiot!'

That's a bit harsh! 'I'm only acting the way that Jenny acts. You don't seem to think that she's an idiot.'

'But you're not acting like her. Or at least, you are, but that's not you.'

'Just because I'm not into playing football any more—'

'You know what, Gwynnie? It's pretty obvious why you're doing all this. Charlie is a good bloke. But if Charlie doesn't like you, then I wouldn't worry about it. You shouldn't try to change yourself for him.'

I say nothing. Guilty as charged. The thing is, I just can't believe that Charlie would ever like the old me. The me that only wore trainers, my brother's T-shirts, no make-up and only knew about football and computer games. The other thing is that I don't even think I am that person any more.

'Whatever.' I need to change the subject now before it gets too deep. 'You meeting up with Jenny later?'

'I doubt it,' he says, 'seeing as we're not going out any more.'

'What?!' This is almost as bad as the fact that I can't go to prom. 'I just spoke to Jenny

and she never said. Why didn't you say anything?'

'Well, she only just dumped me about five
minutes ago. And you have been going on about
your stuff and I haven't been able to get a word
in . . . Anyway, I don't want to talk about it.'

God, I am the worst friend ever. I have been
so wrapped up in myself that Jenny hasn't even
been able to tell me that she wanted to break up
with Paul, and Paul hasn't been able to tell me
that he's just been dumped by Jenny. If they had
then maybe I would have been able to stop it.

'Do you want to get back with her?'

Paul sort of gulps a little and I can tell he's
about to cry, which is so sad because I haven't
seen Paul cry since he was seven and his mum
accidentally put his Pokémon cards in the
wash.

'Right. Leave it to me. I am about to turn you
into the best boyfriend a girl could ever want.
Then you are going to show up at prom and
knock Jenny's popsocks off, and then she will be
desperate to go out with you again.'

It's time for *me* to play fairy godmother.

Thirty minutes later and Paul looks like a new
man. We're back at my house, in Kevin's room.

Paul's wearing Kev's best suit, which is a little big for him but looks pretty cool. I've slicked his hair back with a little bit of Kev's gel so he now looks like a posh gent on his way to a ball. And we manage to find the old aftershave that Kevin had in the back of his cupboard. It's stale, but it still smells better than Paul normally does. Paul's admiring himself in the mirror and he likes what he sees.

I tell him what he needs to do: the flowers, the poem, the DJ playing their song.

'But everyone will laugh at me,' he groans.

'And that will just prove to Jenny how much you care. The more humiliating, the more she'll appreciate it. You know how Jenny likes her PDAs.'

'Her what?'

I roll my eyes like everyone should know that. Then I realize that I am supposed to be nice to Paul right now. 'It means, *Public Displays of Affection*.'

'Yes, she does.' Paul can see my logic. But he doesn't like it. 'At least you'll be there as moral support.'

My face falls. 'Sorry, mate. You're on your own with this one.'

'Oh yeah, I forgot you got tickets to the final. You jammy dodger.'

'How did you know that?'

'It's all your dad can talk about. I've known for ages but he made me promise not to tell. He's so pleased that he's got tickets, and it's like he's especially happy because he gets to go with you. He was saying all that *quality time with his daughter* stuff.'

'Parents are weird, aren't they?'

'Really weird.'

Anyway, whatever. I've given Paul his ammunition to get his girlfriend back. I'll talk Paul up to Jenny. They'll get together again. I'll go to the match with Dad. Then I will have such good karma points that Tottenham will win the final and when we get home Charlie will ask me to be his girlfriend. I am a good person again and I have that happy glowing feeling that I have heard so much about.

But why hasn't Charlie texted me back yet?

chapter 26

'Hi, Gwynnie!'

'Hi, Brianna!' I reply, after realizing that I am the only person with a name as silly as mine, and Brianna Andel from Year 10 was just talking to me.

'Listen,' she says, 'a friend of mine is having a party in a few weeks. You should come. And, like, bring Charlie if you want.'

'Er . . . OK. Thanks!' Did a Year 10 just ask me to a Year 10 party?

'How do you know Brianna Andel from Year 10?' asks Elizabeth, who's walking down the hall with me.

'I don't. I didn't. I've never spoken to her. I didn't even know she knew my name.'

'You're so popular since Charlie asked you to prom in front of everyone.' She frowns like she's thinking something through. 'Gwynnie . . .' she

says, and I'm always suspicious when people start
a sentence with my name.

'Yes.'

Her voice is small. 'Maybe if you tell the
other girls about this party they'll let you rejoin
the BB Club.'

I turn to her and frown. 'I'm not sure I want
to be in the BB Club after they chucked me out
for one little – OK, well, one *huge* – mistake.'

'I'm meeting the other girls for lunch in room
36. I could text them and ask if you can come.'

'I don't need their permission to go into room
36. And even if I did, I wouldn't want to go.'

Elizabeth holds my hand and I wonder
how long it's been since someone has held my
hand. Maybe not since I was a kid and it was a
prerequisite of crossing a road. She looks me
in the eye. 'But *I* want you to be in the BB Club
again. Melissa's pretty nice when she's not
around Kimba, and Tanya just repeats what
everyone else says. But sometimes Jenny makes
me feel . . . and Kimba can be . . . I'm sure she
doesn't mean to be, but Kimba's . . . um . . . a
bit horrible sometimes.' Elizabeth is finding it hard
to say something negative, even about Kimba,
which is bizarre when there's so much to choose

from. 'They are my friends . . . but I only want to hang round them if you're around too.'

'I don't know, Elizabeth,' I say.

'Come on. Please. I'll text them now and tell them that you got an invite to Brianna's party.' She doesn't give me a chance to answer as she starts tapping away with one hand and dragging me off down the hall with the other, through lots of smiles and waves from passing students. I feel like the Queen. I realize that to help out Elizabeth I might have to give the BB Club another chance.

We push our way into room 36 and they are all there.

'Heya, Gwynnie, how's it going?' says Kimba. Which is the nicest thing she has ever said to me. 'You look really pretty today.' No, *that* was the nicest thing she's ever said to me! She must be sorry for being such a cow and chucking me off the Prom Planning Committee.

'Thanks. I'm OK, thanks.'

'Good. I'm so glad to hear it.'

Melissa also has this sympathetic look on her face. 'Jenny told us that you can't come to prom because your dad won't let you. That fully sucks.'

'I know,' I reply. 'It's such a coincidence; I wouldn't be able to be on the Prom Planning

Committee even if you guys hadn't banned me.' I'm reminding them what they did, and I add, 'Be careful what you wish for, hey?'

They all scrunch up their faces like they have no idea what I am talking about.

'So, um, did you get an invite to the Year 10 party that's on in a couple of weeks?' asks Kimba.

'Yeah, it was the weirdest—'

'Do you think you could get us in?'

'I don't see why not. But,' I say, 'that's not why I'm here, is it?'

Tanya looks a little shy while Melissa says, 'Of course not! We just wanted to see if you were OK. You know, after having blown it with Charlie and everything.'

I know that might not be true but I can't put up a front when it comes to Charlie. 'I am so upset. Charlie is my one true soulmate. Going to the prom with him would have been my dream. And it was going to happen. And now it isn't.'

'That's the saddest thing I have ever heard,' says Tanya, and she squeezes my shoulder.

'Thanks. I feel like it's the end of things between me and him. He asked me in front of everyone and now I've turned him down.'

'Men don't handle it so well when you hurt their ego,' says Jenny. 'They find it hard to bounce back, and then— Elizabeth, are you crying?'

We all turn to Elizabeth and she has got tears in her eyes. 'It's so awful!' she wails. 'He loves you and you love him and now you can't be together because your father won't allow it. It's worse than *Romeo and Juliet*!'

'Come on, Elizabeth, don't cry.' I stroke her arm in a soothing way. 'It's probably not *that* bad, given that my dad will let me go out with Charlie eventually, he just wants me to go to this thing on Saturday.'

But all Elizabeth can do is sob.

'And no one is planning to take any poison.'

We all agree that it's not quite as bad as *Romeo and Juliet*, but it's right up there.

'So,' asks Jenny, 'did he text back in the end?'

'Yeah, eventually.' I get out my phone and find the text. I must have looked at it about 300 times since he sent it. 'It says: *gutted ☹ we wld have had fun. c u round x x.* What do you think he meant?'

They all take it in turns to have a look at the text. This is harder than balancing chemical equations and we all sit in silence for a minute as we try to work it out.

'Well,' says Tanya, deep in thought, '*have fun* probably meant spending the whole night snogging. Maybe he would have felt under your top too.'

'Oooooh yeah.' (The consensus of the group.)

'But, then again,' Melissa points out, '*see you around* sounds a little dismissive.' She's right. It does sound dismissive. 'It could be that he's had enough of you and never wants to see you around ever.'

Charlie never wants to see me again.

'But,' Elizabeth says, 'that's totally cancelled out by the two kisses!'

There's hope.

'The thing is,' says Jenny, 'sometimes people put kisses on the end of texts by accident, so they might mean nothing.'

'Hmmm.' This has given us all something to think about.

I guess I have to forgive the BB Club. They are being so nice, counselling me over the loss of Charlie. For the next two days we spend lunch hours, morning breaks and MSN sessions talking about his text, and we're still none the wiser.

'Can we talk about something else now,

please?' asks Jenny. 'I think I know every pixel of that text by heart. It's not going to give us any more clues.'

'Fair enough,' I say. And it is. I have been kind of hogging the conversation topic for a while. 'I guess you guys need to talk about prom. How are those last-minute arrangements going?'

'Real good,' says Melissa.

'Oh great!' I say, trying not to sound too surprised. 'You've finalized the decorations then?'

'Not exactly,' says Kimba, 'but most of us have a date now.'

Tanya looks sad. 'I still haven't managed to persuade my mum to let me go.'

Kimba carries on like she hasn't heard. 'Richard Williams asked me to go with him.'

I always thought Richard Williams had more sense.

Melissa says, 'Well, he's only a Year 9. I'm going with Jimmy Noble from Year 10.'

'Yeah,' says Kimba, 'but then again, you *are* a Year 10, so really you should be going with a boy from Year 11.'

'What about you, Elizabeth?' I ask.

Elizabeth blushes and I feel bad for asking. She must not have been asked by anyone.

'Don't be horrible, Gwynnie,' says Melissa, 'no one has asked—'

But Elizabeth interrupts her. 'Actually . . . um, Ranjit asked me to go.'

We all stand there gobsmacked for a moment.

'And I said yes.' She looks worried as none of us have found the words to speak. 'Should I have said yes?'

'Yes!' I shout. 'That's great news. You and Ranj make a brilliant couple.' I'm not shocked that he's asked Elizabeth, more that Ranj has asked anyone!

Kimba makes a face to Melissa likes she's not so sure, but luckily Elizabeth is too busy beaming to notice. 'Good. Because I think I like him a little bit.'

'I knew it!' I say. 'How did he ask you?'

'Well, we bonded over fizzy cola bottles,' she says, giving me a quick smile.

'Well, if there is a way to a man's heart, it's artificial flavourings and E-numbers,' I say. But then I catch Jenny's eye and she looks all sad and left out of the conversation. Since she's broken up with Paul she doesn't have a date. 'I'm sorry, Jenny. All we're talking about is boys and you don't have one.'

'Well, I am still going to go to prom.'

'That's very brave of you,' I say, and everyone *hmm*s in agreement.

She nods a thanks and a sort of sniff, which I figure is holding back a sob. 'You're my true pals.'

I am her true pal, but I wish more than anything that *I* was going to prom this weekend instead of her. When she doesn't even have a date and I do . . . er . . . did. But instead I'll be in a car, heading down to London, and miles away from Charlie Notts, the most perfect Year 10 boy that has ever walked the planet, and one that was even crazy enough to like me.

chapter 27

It's the big day. The day that was supposed to be prom night and is now FA Cup final day.

We're driving to London in the car Dad's borrowed from Angela — well, I suppose he's allowed to, seeing as they are secretly dating . . . OK that's still just a hunch. Meanwhile, all the BB girls are decorating the hall for prom, doing their hair and nails and make-up and putting on their dresses ready to have the best night of their lives.

'Let's sing, shall we, Gwyndoe?'

'Dad! We're not even out of Northampton yet,' I point out.

The worst thing is that Dad is so unbelievably happy. He's been humming and whistling since he told me he'd got the tickets. I have to pretend to be happy too, which makes the fact that I really don't want to be here so much worse.

'♫ *Oh when the Spurs* ♫ . . . Come on, Gwynnie . . . ♫ *Go marching in* ♫ Come on!'

'I don't know the words.'

He laughs. 'What do you mean, you don't know the words? ♫ *Oh when the Spurs go marching in* ♫ . . . Now you.'

'♫ *I want to be in that number* ♫ . . .'

He is so excited that he cannot tell that I am only whispering.

'♫ *OH WHEN THE SPURS GO MARCHING IN* ♫!! Oi, oi!' My dad is yelling at the top of his lungs; whacking the car roof with his hand as he sings. He's like an eight-year-old. He sees another carload of Tottenham supporters and beeps at them. They beep back and wave. It's like the whole world is happy except me.

'So, Gwynnie, I've heard that Charlie fellow is a nice lad?' He phrases it like a question so I have to answer.

'He's OK.'

'He's a little bit older than you, isn't he?'

'Only in the year above,' I say all defensively, in case he won't let me go out with him and we do end up like Romeo and Juliet.

'When I was at school, all the girls wanted to

go out with the boys in the year above. Is that still the case?'

'I suppose so.' I could just leave it at that, but I feel I need to educate my dad about boys in the twenty-first century. 'The guys in our year are so immature.'

'But the guys in the year above are mature, are they?'

'Some of them are. Charlie is. He's just really nice and funny and not completely obsessed with football and computers and stuff.' Oh God, how did I let that slip out?

'Really? So he's nice *and* funny, is he?' Dad's smirking now. 'But he's got to like football too though. I wouldn't allow you to go out with a rugby fan.'

I nod my head.

'And what team does he support? If you say Arsenal, I will ban you from seeing him.'

'No . . .' I wait to drop the killer blow. 'He's a Spurs fan.'

'Gwynnie, you have found a winner! Does he know you're coming today? What am I talking about? I bet you've been bragging to your mates about this all week.'

I don't say anything.

We pull into a car park and my dad pays more than a tenner to park here. This trip must be costing him a fortune. He should have taken someone else.

He gets out of the car and just stands there gazing up at the weird archway things that hang over Wembley. He sighs. 'This is it, luv. This is the real thing. I have never seen Spurs play in a final for anything and now I am. It's a dream come true.' I hold back the tears as he puts his arm around me. 'Isn't it marvellous? Wembley Stadium . . . Just imagine what all your friends are doing right now—'

Suddenly I burst into tears. And not just trickling-elegantly-down-your-face tears, but loud humongous sobs so bad I can't even breathe any more.

'Gwynnie, what's the matter, luv?'

'I want . . . I didn't . . . I don't . . .' I can't even get a sentence out, and even if I could I wouldn't know what to say or how to say it.

Dad looks really worried. 'All right, little one. Take a deep breath.'

I breathe in. I breathe out. It doesn't really help. I just can't find a way to make this OK. 'It's Spurs . . . And you really want it . . . But

Charlie . . . And the prom, I mean, prom . . . And everyone . . . But it's the final . . . And you have spent all this money . . . But I really like him . . .'

'Gwynnie, slow down, darling. What are you trying to say?'

'I'm so sorry, Dad.'

Dad just gives me a hug and lets me cry for a bit, which is really nice. 'Gwyndoe, what do you have to be sorry for?'

'I still love Spurs, Dad, I really do. But today is prom and everyone is going and Charlie Notts asked me to go with him and I had to say I couldn't go because I was coming here.'

'Oh.'

'Now Charlie will fancy someone else and I can't believe he ever fancied me in the first place!'

'I see.'

'And you've spent all this money on the tickets and coming down here and everything, and now I'm just being an unpleasant kid and I've ruined your big day.' I can't work out Dad's face, but I'm pretty sure that he must hate me right now. 'I'm so sorry, Dad. I'll stop crying in a second and then we can go in. I'll be fine in a second.' But I know that I won't.

Dad looks into the distance somewhere for ages. When he looks back down at me he has tears in his eyes too. 'I'm the one that should be sorry, luv. I wanted to do something nice for you, but I got it wrong. You want to go to this prom thing—'

'No, it's fine, Dad. I don't want to go any more.'

'I wanted to do something nice for your fourteenth birthday, and instead of getting you what you wanted I thought you were still a little girl—'

'No, really, Dad, it's OK. Even if I did go, I don't have the right hair or make-up or outfit. Let's just watch the match. Prom will be rubbish anyway.'

'And with an attitude like that, how are we ever going to make Charlie Motts fall in love with you?'

I giggle in a snotty way. 'It's Charlie *Notts*, Dad.'

'Motts, Notts, who cares?! He's possibly the only Spurs supporter of your generation left in the whole world. If we don't nab him now we might lose him forever.'

'But, Dad, how—'

'Leave it to me.' He squeezes my shoulders. 'Gwynderella, you shall go to the ball!' My dad is the best, but it still doesn't mean he's got any funnier. 'Don't move.'

I see him walk off towards some really dodgy-looking men who are hanging around in the car park. He talks to one of them for a minute, then comes back with a fistful of cash.

'Where did you get that from?'

'I sold the tickets.'

'But, Dad, those tickets were your dream come true. How could you have sold them?'

'Aw, Gwynnie –' he hugs me again and sniffs – 'I would do anyth . . .' Then he stops and shakes himself like a dog coming out of the rain, like he's shaking off his disappointment. 'Have some faith in the boys, will you? Spurs will win again next year. But for now, we have some stuff to do.'

'Like go back home and get ready for prom?'

'No. Like find a swanky hair-do-ist to do your hair, and nails and make-up and stuff, buy you a fancy dress to wear, then get back to that prom and get your Prince Charming!'

*

Vidal Sassoon in Oxford Street in London is the best hairdressers in the world. They trimmed my hair, curled it, styled it and made me look like a model. And Dad paid to get my nails done too.

We come out of the salon and Dad starts running towards the parking meter that costs like five pounds an hour to park at. 'Right, let's go get you a dress.'

'Dad, it's almost four o'clock. There's no way we can buy a dress and get back in time.'

'I had no idea that women's hair took so long. I've never had a hair appointment that lasted more than twenty minutes.'

'Don't worry. Do you remember the dress that's in the cupboard?'

Dad looks confused. He's never seen me in a dress.

'Um. The one that belonged to Mum.' I realize that I should have checked with him first. 'Do you mind?'

Dad's face is not what I expected. He's smiling and he doesn't look sad at all. 'You'll look lovely in that, Gwynnie.'

We get into the car and race back to Northampton. I can't wait for everyone to see how brilliant I look, and I have already planned out how I will accessorize Mum's dress so that it won't look so old-fashioned. Luckily the eighties are back.

'Dad . . .' I say really slowly so that he knows I mean it, 'if you want to marry Angela Shields I don't mind. And I'm sure Mum wouldn't either. Angela's great.'

Dad looks completely shocked. 'Where's this come from?'

'I know you're seeing each other. You're always round there all the time. You say you're going for tea and stuff, but I'm not a kid any more. If you want to, like, go out with her, that's fine. And I'm sure Paul feels the same. He thinks you're pretty cool.' I can't let that one go without saying anything. 'Paul's clearly mental.'

'Well, I'm glad to know that I have your permission.'

'That's OK, Dad. It's about time you moved on.'

'What I mean is: it's good to know that I have your permission, but I am not seeing Angela, and I'm not interested in seeing Angela. We're just friends.'

'It's OK, Dad, I don't mind.'

'I can tell you don't. But what I'm telling you is that we're just friends.'

'Then why are you round there all the time recently?'

Dad looks shifty and I think he's about to finally come out with it. 'Well . . .' I bet he's glad that he can look at the road and not at me right now. 'The thing is, I needed some extra cash and Angela needed some stuff done in her garden and she's been paying me a bit to do it for her.'

'For the Spurs tickets . . .' Now I feel really bad. 'You worked extra hard for those tickets and you've wasted the day in a girlie beauty parlour.'

'Are you kidding? I've had great fun! I have found out what a French manicure is, when I always thought it was a medical remedy for continental males.' I give him the *very funny, Dad* look. 'And now I have uncovered the mystery as to what those strange utensils in your bedroom are. I thought they were heated chopsticks.' He's talking about my hair straighteners and there's no way he thought they were heated chopsticks (although heated chopsticks are a brilliant idea!).

'Besides, I got to spend the day with my favourite girl in the world.'

Dad's being cheesy so I put a stop to it. 'I didn't see Cameron Diaz out with us today.'

Dad gives me the *very funny* look like I've just given him. 'Ha ha.'

I wait a second before I ask, 'So you're not with Paul's mum then?'

'No. I promise. Men and women can just be friends you know.'

'I know.' I say it like it's obvious. But really I am relieved. And my dad might be the best dad in the world — buying me FA Cup final tickets. Selling those tickets. Sitting through a makeover when he could have been sitting through an important match. I should probably tell him how great he is.

'Dad.'

'Yeah.'

'You're all right, you know.'

He grins from ginger sideburn to ginger sideburn. 'Thanks, Gwynnie. You're not so bad yourself.'

And I smile from tonged ringlet to tonged ringlet.

*

We get to the house at 7 p.m., and I've got about a millisecond until we have to turn around and head back out to prom, which starts at half seven, but I know the BB girls said they were going to be fashionably late and get there at quarter to eight. Dad stops outside and I jump out before he even has time to put the handbrake on.

I open the door and I can hear giggling. 'Hello?' I call. I'm always afraid that one day a burglar will answer. But today's not that day.

Kevin calls back, 'Hello?' He sounds as if he's been taken by surprise, which is odd because usually he can hear people coming from fifty miles away. He sticks his head round the living-room door and he looks all messy and kind of sleepy. 'What are you doing here?' he says. 'I thought you were at the match.'

Dad's made it in from outside. 'Something more important came up. Hi, son, what's going on?'

Kev looks a bit sheepish and says, 'I thought I'd show my girlfriend where I grew up.'

'Is that so?'

'What could be more important than the FA

Cup final?' Kev's trying to change the subject.

'I've got to get ready for prom,' I tell him. 'I've only got twenty minutes to put on my make-up and my dress—'

A girl's voice comes from inside the living room. 'Ooooh, prom! Can I help?' Stephanie Gregson pops her head round the door. She also looks a bit messy and her top is buttoned up wrong. 'I'm the queen of make-up!'

'Dad, Gwynnie, this is Stephanie. Stephanie, this is my sister, Gwynnie, and my dad, Michael.'

'Lovely to meet you, Stephanie . . . at last,' Dad says. 'Anyone would think that Kevin was embarrassed of us, the way that he's been hiding you. He must have psychically known that we were going to miss the match today.'

Dad's taking the mick, but I have no time for that either. 'Thanks, Stephanie, I'd love your help!' This is fantastic – I have wicked hair, fab nails and I am about to get my make-up done by the girl with the best make-up in the whole of Northampton.

Upstairs Stephanie sits me down in front of a mirror while Kevin is put to work making me a sandwich and Dad is in charge of ironing Mum's dress. 'You have such beautiful skin, Gwynnie,' Stephanie says. 'You shouldn't pile on the make-up.' She starts dabbing me with a brush. 'Did you know that I was the one helped your brother pick this out?'

'I didn't know, but thank you. It's great stuff.'

'You're welcome.' She knows we're running late so she hurries. 'Now, unfortunately we don't have time to apply any fake tan, but I do have some bronzer. I can't live without it. Especially as we always spend Easter in rainy Bognor Regis with my nan and crazy Aunt Maxwell.'

'Your aunt is called Maxwell?'

'Don't ask.'

Suddenly the penny drops. 'Hang on a minute – did you not go to America for Easter?'

'No. Why?'

'No reason.' Jenny is probably too embarrassed to say about not going to California, just like I'm too embarrassed to say about the football stuff. We'll have to have a proper spill session. Then we'll be close, like twin sisters. Or closer.

Stephanie does my make-up. It's not so much

that I look like a tart, but just enough so you can tell I've made an effort.

Dad comes in with the dress all ironed perfectly. 'Gwynnie, you look gorgeous. I can't believe—'

'Dad,' I cut in, 'if you say the words *grown up* or *woman* I might properly vom all over myself. And then I'll have to redo my make-up, and frankly we just don't have the time.'

'Fair enough.' He hands the dress over and buttons his lip. 'I'd better leave you grown-up women to it then.'

I throw a pillow at him on his way out.

'Stephanie, do you mind if I do this bit by myself, please?'

She nods and leaves the room.

I pick up Mum's dress from where Dad has placed it on the bed. It's a baby-blue colour that really brings out the grey in my eyes. Mum had the same eyes as me. I remember them. I put the dress on back to front and button up the back before sliding it round so it's in the right place. It's a sort of strapless boob tube on top and the skirt bit has a million layers of light blue chiffon so that it puffs out like a tutu. In the layers of chiffon are little diamonds that sparkle when I move. I know what word Jenny would use to describe this dress: *timeless and classy*. OK, that's two words.

Finally, I look in the mirror.

I look gorgeous.

chapter 28

It's quarter past eight as Dad pulls up outside school, but I am no longer worried about time; it'll start when I get there.

'Now, remember, I'm picking you up at eleven thirty, Gwynnie.'

'Eleven thirty?' OK, maybe I do have to worry about time. 'Dad, I'm not a child . . . and this is prom. Can't I stay till midnight?'

'Fine then, midnight. But not a second later.'

'You're still the best, Dad. Thanks.'

'Have fun, Gwynnie. And make sure you get a snog from that Charlie boy.'

'*Dad!*' I look around to see if anyone heard, but luckily everyone is already inside.

I walk away, before remembering something. 'Dad?'

'Yeah.'

'How did Spurs do?'

'Do you know what, Gwynnie? I forgot to check.'

My dad is the worst liar in the world. 'You'd be more likely to forget Christmas day than Spurs in the final!' I say. 'Go on. How'd we do?'

He breaks into the biggest smile. 'We killed them! 3–2!' He goes into full football chant mode, '♫ COME ON, YOU SPURS! ♫'

This is the best news ever. I feel bad that we missed it but so glad that we won. I'm about to apologize again but he stops me.

'Go on, Gwynnie. You're late enough as it is!' He smiles at me and tells me to knock 'em dead.

I walk through the playground towards the hall. I can hear muffled music and people talking really loudly. I feel properly nervous because either Charlie is going to ask me out tonight or I am going to ask him. There are loads of people hanging around in the big corridor outside the hall. I can see Francesca Ramsgate and Justin Kark; they obviously came together but wish that they hadn't as they're just standing there not talking or anything. Rachel Govens and Asher Quinn are there, holding hands, and I'm sure that Rachel is thinking that she really wants him to snog her, and it looks like he wants to snog her too but he doesn't know how to start. I see two people snogging but I can't tell who they are as their faces are stuck together. Then I realize that it's Elizabeth and Ranj! I am so happy for them.

Elizabeth breaks away from him to inhale and sees me. She smiles like an absolute loon and I smile back at her and give her the thumbs-up. She gives me the thumbs-up back and makes a *Wow, you look gorgeous* face, all mouth opened and shocked. Ranjit turns around to see who she is looking at and sort of blushes when he sees it's me. 'Hey, Gwynnie. You look nice.' High praise, coming from Ranj.

'Not as nice as Elizabeth though,' I reply with a wink.

He blushes again.

'We thought you weren't coming,' says Elizabeth, looking a little distracted.

'Yeah, well, I managed to get out of the th—' but then I can't be bothered to pretend to explain. 'Where is everyone?'

'Last time I saw Melissa she was shouting at Jimmy Noble because he was refusing to dance with her. Tanya's mum did let her come after all and she is snogging Robin Hall at the back somewhere. Kimba is looking for Richard Williams, who seems to have given her the slip.'

'It appears he does have some sense after all.'

Elizabeth does her piglet laugh and it makes Ranjit smile. She can't quite bring herself to say anything actually mean, but she totally agrees with me.

I don't want to be too obvious, but there is no way to ask without just asking. 'Have you seen Charlie? I need to let him know that he's not a complete dateless fool.'

'Er . . . no . . . I haven't seen either of them . . . sorry.' What does she mean, *either of them*? But before I can ask Ranjit has grabbed her for another snog and she's stuck to his face again. Which I suppose is fair enough.

I walk along to the main entrance of the big hall. Everyone is staring at me. They're all saying, 'You look great, Gwynnie,' and it gives me confidence. 'Thank you. You look nice too.'

The thing is, there is something else, something weird behind their looks that makes me feel a little paranoid, like they know something I don't. Maybe Charlie has been sobbing about the fact that I couldn't be here and they are waiting to see the look of surprise on his face. Oh God, maybe he decided not to come and they know that I will be left disappointed. I knew I should have texted him!

I put one foot inside the hall – it looks amazing! I would hardly recognize it. The BB girls have done a great job. It's completely covered with white sheets so it looks like a marquee and you can't see all the school stuff on the walls. There are pink-and-white balloons and pink-and-white streamers everywhere. There's even a disco mirror ball on the ceiling like I suggested. Fairy lights hit the mirror ball and make the place all twinkly. Basically, it looks like the films I used to watch with my mum – really cool. The stage is all lit up and Stephanie's DJ friend is playing wicked music. There aren't that many people dancing; it's just a few girls together. The boys are standing round the edges, but it's still early. I can't wait to slow-dance with Charlie. If he's even here.

Then I see him. He's wearing black trousers and a black shirt, open at the collar. He looks even better than he does every day. Which is pretty good. He hasn't seen me though. Is it too weird if I just watch him for a minute? Yes, it probably is. 'Charlie Notts!' I blurt. *Charlie* would probably have been better.

'Er, Gwynnie. Hi,' Charlie sort of stammers. 'You made it.'

'Yes.' He's glad that I've made it. This is brilliant. It's all going according to plan . . . the plan which I have just made up.

'Why aren't you off being a bridesmaid?'

What is he talking about? Oh yeah, bridesmaid. 'Er . . .' Think quick. Not exactly to plan. Not a problem, I'll wing it. 'The wedding finished early.'

'But, wasn't it in Scotland?'

'Yes . . . but we flew . . . Er, and there was the time difference.'

'From Scotland?'

My rubbishly bad get-out lie isn't what we should be concentrating on right now. 'Look, forget about my cousin's wedding—'

'Second cousin,' Charlie says.

'Second cousin's wedding.'

'Twice removed.'

'Yes, him – er, I mean – her. Just forget about it. I need to ask you something.' I can't wait another minute to ask him. If I don't get it out now then I might explode. Which would totally ruin my mum's perfect dress.

'What?' He's looking around at everything but me.

'It's something that I've wanted to ask you for a while.' I step towards him. 'Something I hoped you would ask me . . . and I thought you were going to . . .' I look deep in his eyes and try to look earnest. (It would help if I knew what earnest meant.) '. . . but I thought I would make it easier on the both of us by saying it first . . . I think you know what I am going to say.'

'Gwy—'

'Hang on, Charlie.' Now that I have worked my confidence up to it I don't want him to steal the thunder and ask me before I can ask him. 'We've been friends since you started at this school. A lot has changed since then,' (like my dress sense) 'but a lot has stayed the same . . .' (like I'm still totally in love with you).

Out of the corner of my eye I see Paul come in from outside. He's wearing my brother's suit, and his hair is all slicked back just like I showed him. He has a flower in his lapel and he's even carrying a humongous bunch of red roses. Apart from the fact he's the colour of milk, and he's sweating like a marathon runner in a mascot costume, he looks pretty good . . . for Paul.

The words of our football coach ring in my ears: *Focus, you moron!* Right now is not about Paul. 'You see, um, Charlie—'

But I can't stop looking at Paul. He's the only guy in here that has put any effort into how he looks and it makes him seem a bit weird. I was the one who told him to do all this. Does that mean I should help him through his nerves?

'You see, Charlie . . .'

Paul looks over at me with wide, panicky eyes. But I turn away from him. I'll have to chat to Paul later, when I am Charlie's girlfriend and we're taking a rest from all the snogging.

Paul walks off into the hall and so I am left alone with Charlie.

'Charlie . . .' Here goes. 'I really like you. And not just in a friend way.'

'Wow, Gwynnie.'

'I was so happy when you asked me to prom because tonight will be the perfect night for us to get together properly.'

Charlie goes all shy and cute. 'I didn't realize—'

But then suddenly Tanya comes running up to us. 'Everyone! Paul is about to do a sketch or sing a song or something.'

I'm waiting to seal the girlfriend deal with Charlie, but we're sort of ushered into the hall by the people going to see what Paul has to say. *Hold that thought, Charlie.*

I'm in the hall, and there's Paul getting up on stage next to the DJ. I've lost Charlie in the crowd, but at least I'm here for Paul's PDA. Everyone in the whole school goes quiet and turns and stares at him. I hope this works. Then Tanya whispers to me. 'You look so great, Gwynnie.'

'Thanks, Tanya. You too.'

'And it's so brave of you to come . . . . given everything that's happened.'

'Given everything that's happened when?'

But she doesn't answer. Paul's on the microphone and is about to speak. 'Errrr . . . I . . . errr. Hello. Errr, hi, everyone.'

Paul is not an excellent public speaker. He gets out a sheet of paper. He's written a speech. A long one. I realize now that this could go horribly, horribly wrong. There's a chance that I might have made a big mistake — worse than a white bra with a black top — and Paul's paying for it.

'I just wanted to say that I hope you are having a good time.' He pauses as if waiting for a round of applause, but no one makes a sound. Poor Paul. 'And . . . um . . . I also wanted to say something else.' Everything is deathly quiet. I know Paul is hating this, but if he gets Jenny back it'll all be worth it. If he doesn't, this will be worse than me and the uniform and Elizabeth and the Incident rolled into one. 'I've been going out with the most wonderful girl in the whole world these past two months. She is beautiful and nice and funny and special and I think that I am in love with her.'

People start laughing. This is really awkward.

'Jennifer Gregson?' He looks around for her in the audience but can't see her. 'Jenny, where are you?' Everyone in the hall is looking for Jenny now.

Jenny puts her hand up at the other side of the hall and steps forward. She's looking fab in this floor-length sequinned pink halterneck that matches the colour scheme of the room and shows off her enhanced boobs. She also has this cool pink-and-white feathery fascinator in her hair. But she doesn't look pleased about being the centre of attention this time. She looks embarrassed.

'Jenny, I got you flowers. And, this poem is for you:

> These roses are red
> Chelsea wear blue
> You're totally amazing
> And I really love you.

> When I'm playing on Xbox
> My fave's Gears of War
> I promise to listen
> And talk to you more.

> Goalies wear green
> Refs wear black
> I'll love you for ever
> Will you please take me back?

'I wrote it myself.'

Someone calls out from the audience. 'No, really?'

More laughter.

Oh no, Paul's got more to say. Why won't he stop talking? 'I'm sorry if I've been a rubbish boyfriend and not put you first and paid you enough attention and stuff, but if you take me back I promise to be a better boyfriend and love you more and do nothing but call you and text you and take you out to Nando's whenever I have enough money.' Paul seems to be feeling a little more confident now that he's nearing the end of his speech. 'I've asked the DJ to play our song.' He signals to the DJ. I think he's expecting him to bring in the tune in a seamless way, but he doesn't. He sort of fiddles around a bit with some buttons and stuff. This is going about as smoothly as chunky peanut butter. Everyone is properly laughing at Paul now. I have just realized that Jenny might have thought she wanted this, but in reality Paul looks like a muppet, and nobody wants to go out with a muppet. Eventually *Breaking Free* from High School Musical starts ringing through the air. Paul gets to the edge of the stage and finishes up with, 'Jenny, will you go out with me again and dance with me to our song?'

He drops the mic, jumps off the stage and walks towards her. Everyone is still looking. It's like something out of a film. Or it would be except Jenny's face is flaming and clashing with her pink dress. Hopefully she'll be embarrassed but also realize that Paul is a nice guy and is doing this to impress her. Even if it's not that impressive.

I have to see what happens, but I can't get near enough as everyone is crowding round, also wanting to see.

I am about twelve people back and I get a glimpse of Paul approaching Jenny and trying to scoop her up in his arms like I told him to. Trouble is, he's not quite strong enough. He sort of grabs her leg and lifts her a millimetre off the floor. But he sticks to his script. 'We're soaring, Jenny, we're flying.' Oh no, he's incorporated lines from the song! 'You are the only woman in the world for me. Will you be my girl?'

All eyes are on Jenny. Including mine.

'No.' She can't quite look at him. 'Sorry, Paul, but I can't.'

This is terrible news. Paul looks crushed. He drops Jenny the millimetre back down again. He looks worse than when he spent a total of fifty-eight hours getting to the last level of *Tour of Duty* and then the computer crashed and he couldn't save it. He can't quite believe it, not after he's gone to all this effort. 'Why?' His voice cracks.

'Um. I've found someone else.'

Everyone goes 'Oooooooh,' in a mean sort of way because they know that's got to hurt.

Who's Jenny found? How come I don't know about this? Is it that Year 11 bloke she says is always looking at her? Maybe she's lying to make Paul feel better that she's turning him down. Looking at him, I don't think it's worked.

Paul legs it off somewhere. Everyone is too shocked to even laugh at him. People are going to be talking about this for years. Poor Paul.

Jenny stands there for a bit, looking upset too. She goes off the other way. I'd better follow her; she probably needs to talk to me. I am her best friend after all.

I dodge my way through the crowd trying to find her. She is quite easy to follow because I just have to look in the direction everyone's heads have turned. But I'm at the back of the hall now and I can't see her anywhere. Hang on a minute— is that her in the corner? Is that her kissing some bloke? I guess it wasn't a lie then, she's got a new boyfriend already. Who is it? The two faces pull apart.

Oh my God.

Jenny is kissing Charlie Notts.

chapter 29

Why am I so completely stupid?

I'm watching my so-called best friend kiss the boy that I have been in love with since the moment I saw him. The boy I was just in the middle of asking to be my boyfriend. I can't believe that I didn't see what a bitch Jenny Gregson was all this time, and that Charlie was just using me to get to her.

I stomp over to them with my hands on my hips, all buzzing with indignity (if that's the right word). I don't know who to shout at first. 'Hello, you two.'

They manage to stop snogging each other and look at me. They've been caught out.

'What the hell is this?' I shout.

'I thought you weren't coming,' says Charlie, looking guilty.

'Is that why you decided to cheat on me with my best friend?' I ask him.

'Gwynnie! You're here!' Jenny goes from pale to red to pale again.

'Yes, I am,' I say. 'And so are you. Having a great time. With *my* bloke.'

She says nothing.

'How could you?'

'Um.' Her eyes are darting around all over the place. 'It's not as if you and him were going steady.'

'I wasn't talking to you, Jenny. And I wish that you wouldn't speak like that – you're not an American and you don't sound like one.'

There's another 'Ooooooh,' from behind me, and I realize that the whole school is watching. I don't care. Let them watch.

Charlie looks at me and I can see that he's only just taken in my hair and dress. 'Gwynnie, I didn't get the chance to say before, but you look great.'

That kind of floors me for a second because it's so unexpected. It also reminds me how much I like him: absolutely loads. This really hurts. 'How could you do this to me?' I gulp.

'I'm so sorry, Gwynnie. But——' Charlie says.

'I wasn't talking to you, Charlie,' I say. 'I was talking to my *best mate* over here.'

Jenny can't speak. She's just looking at the floor.

Charlie, ever the gentleman, fills in for her. 'But, Gwynnie, she's got a point: you and me weren't going out or anything.'

The annoying thing is, he's right. They both are. I say, 'But you asked me to prom,' in this little pathetic voice, knowing it's futile.

'And I wanted to go with you,' he looks really genuine. So what happened? '. . . as a friend.'

Yuck. *Friend*. The most offensive f-word in the English language.

'You've been so great to me since I came to this school; you talked to me when no one else would. You have been getting more and more bizarre, but I really like hanging out with you, playing football and computer and stuff . . . But I've always had a thing for Jenny——'

Jenny has the decency to stifle her smile.

'How could you prefer Jenny to me?' The pathetic voice is back again. 'She's such a . . . a . . .' I know that everyone is listening and I don't know if I should say what I want to say.

'Such a what?' asks Jenny with a deep frown.

But Charlie answers before I can tell her. 'I

don't know, Gwynnie, sometimes it seems like you're acting like someone who's not you. Like you're pretending. Jenny's real, and you're, I dunno, a little . . . er . . .' He winces.

'What?' I ask. '*Fake?!*'

'Um . . .' He can't think of a less offensive way of saying it.

'Jenny's real, all right.' A voice comes from behind me. It's Elizabeth and she's storming over looking furious. 'A real bitch!'

This time it's a gasp from the audience. No one's ever heard Elizabeth speak like this!

Jenny looks hurt and tries to defend herself. 'I can't help it if I am what you two have to pretend to be. I can't help it if you have to fake it.'

'Jenny, what—' I say, but apparently Elizabeth hasn't finished.

'*Gwynnie* fakes it? What about you? You pretended to like Paul when all the time you liked Charlie, snogging Paul's face off to make Charlie jealous. You pretended to be Gwynnie's friend so that you could get close to all the blokes that were her friends. And as soon as you realized there was a chance Charlie might like her, you tried to ruin it.' The crowd behind us

264

is back on my side and starts jeering in support. Even Charlie has to admit that that doesn't make Jenny look too nice.

'*And* you do this completely fake American slang when you were only there for a couple of weeks!'

Jenny is so shocked she can't speak.

I'm shocked too but I stand next to Elizabeth and back her up. 'Actually,' I say, 'I just found out that you spent your holidays in Bognor Regis with your nan and a crazy aunt named Maxwell.' Howls of laughter erupt from behind me. 'So unless they speak some weird transatlantic dialect in Bognor, you're faking that too.'

Jenny's gone bright red. Charlie can't look at her.

'Come on, Elizabeth!' I say.

Elizabeth and I walk out of the hall, pretending to be calm, but as soon as we're outside the door we start to run. We leg it down the corridor to room 36. It's all dark, but we don't turn the lights on. We can't speak as we both go through in our heads what we've just done.

'Are you OK?' she asks me.

'I don't know. I feel like I've just had forty cans of Red Bull. My mind won't stop moving.' I look at her and can just make out the whites of her eyes. 'Elizabeth, you were amazing!'

'Well,' she says, 'I felt really bad for you, and I thought it was time that Jenny was made to feel as bad as she makes me feel sometimes. She's never been very nice to me.'

'Yeah, well, you were really brave out there.'

We flick our heads round as we hear someone at the door. I assume it's a teacher telling us to get out of the classroom. But it's not. When the person steps closer I can see that it's Jenny. I should have smelled her coming by the Britney perfume mixed with the scent of shame.

She pushes the door open wider. 'Gwynnie, are you in here? I have to speak to you. Can I come in?'

'Free country,' I reply with a shrug.

Elizabeth looks at me and gives my hand a squeeze. Then she leaves the room and leaves us to it.

'Gee,' says Jenny, with tears in her eyes, 'Charlie and I have liked each other for ages.'

None of this makes any sense. 'Then why were you helping me to get him?'

'I was doing it for you.' She approaches me slowly, with her hands out as if I might think she has a grenade or something. 'I've helped make you look better. As a member of the BB Club, and a friend, I wanted to teach you how to make the best of yourself.'

'Well, thanks very much!' I wish *I* had a grenade. But I still have so many questions, which she won't be able to answer if she is blown into a thousand pieces.

'The thing is, Gwynnie –' she pulls the ridiculous fascinator from her head and starts playing with the feathers – 'I was teaching you all this stuff, but actually I wanted to learn from you. You've always been so cool and relaxed around boys. You can go up and talk to them without fear. They all like you and talk to you and you make it so easy for them. If I could get just a bit of that then I would be happy.'

Huh?

'I really liked Charlie from the beginning, and when I thought he was falling for you I got so jealous.' She stops, and stops fiddling with the fascinator. 'I'm sorry, Gee. I've been such a bitch.'

She's right. But I don't even want to agree with her on that. 'Why did you carry on with Paul if you liked Charlie?'

'Paul's OK and everything, but he's only a Year 9. I was waiting for Charlie to make a move, but it turns out that he wouldn't do anything while I was still with Paul. As soon as I knew that Charlie wasn't going with you to prom, I phoned Charlie, told him I'd broken up with Paul and he asked me.'

'Did you tell him you'd broken up with Paul before or after you broke up with Paul?'

'Does it matter?'

'Yes.'

She says nothing and looks at the floor. Charlie has been manipulated by Jenny like a football by a ball-hogging showoff. And he should have known better than to fall for it.

Hang on a minute. Will someone please tell me why I am so completely stupid? I have been wasting my time with Jenny and Charlie when there is someone else that is so much nicer than both of them put together.

'I'm really sorry, Gwynnie. I really do want you to be my friend,' she says.

'Do you know what, Jenny? If you want

Charlie so much, you can have him. I'll get over it.'

She looks hopeful.

'I don't think it's me you should be apologizing to. Right now I've got a genuine friend that I've been rubbish to recently. You haven't been that nice to him either.'

Jenny bites her lip.

'But before that, you should speak to Elizabeth. Tell her you're going to stop treating her like a doormat and start being kind to her from now on.'

Jenny nods.

'And mean it.'

She nods again. I walk out of the room, leaving Jenny alone in the dark. Walking down the corridor I get my phone and text Paul:

Where r u?

After five minutes with no reply I go out to the playground, where I'm pretty sure he'll be. There's a slight chill in the air, and the school buildings look really weird when it's all dark. I call his phone and hear *Blue Is the Colour* — Chelsea's anthem, Paul's ringtone — ringing out everywhere.

I round the corner of the science block and

he's there, looking like the saddest thing that's ever kicked a football. When he sees me come over he stops. I think he's been crying.

'You all right?' I ask.

'I'm OK,' he says, but he's clearly not.

I sigh. 'So. My idea about serenading Jenny didn't go as planned then?'

Even Paul has to smile at this. 'Not quite.'

'I'm sorry, mate.'

'It's all right.'

'No, really. I've been a complete idiot and I'm sorry. I've been obsessed with Charlie Notts and trying to be like Jenny Gregson, when really I should have been trying to be more like me. I mean, Jenny and Charlie are—'

'Do you know what, Gwynnie?'

'What?'

'I don't want to talk about it.'

'Fair enough.' I can understand that. We don't have to talk about everything to be friends, we just have to be there. I've been a bit lame at that these past few weeks and I'm going to get better.

I reach down and take off my heels. 'Come on then: kick-ball. First to three.'

Paul smiles at me and passes the ball. I whack

it at the wall with superb precision and it bounces off, straight to Paul's feet. Luckily it seems I haven't lost it.

chapter 30

Jenny texts:

> *hey G u still angry with me? i no its only been 2 days*
> *but i miss u loads. pls b my friend again.*

Delete.

Charlie texts:

> *hi gwynnie. sorry about Saturday. how r u? at least*
> *spurs won the match!*

Delete.

That was the second text I got from Charlie, and the second one I've deleted. It was the nineteenth from Jenny. Which is a lot, even for her.

Sunday was so rubbish that I didn't even leave my room. But at least Monday was a bank holiday so it gave me more thinking time. Now it's Tuesday morning. So, what to do? Go back to Old Gwynnie, or stick with New, Girlie Gwynnie?

I look at my hair and decide I can't leave the house with it looking like this. I have to straighten it. Then I do my make-up. I make sure my eyeshadow matches my blazer perfectly. I look pretty OK for someone who's had their back stabbed and heart trampled on just forty-eight hours ago.

I get to the bus stop and I see Jenny, Kimba, Melissa, Tanya and even Elizabeth in their usual spot: leaning against the railings of Becket's Park.

'Heya, Gwynnie! We're over here!' Tanya calls me over in her puppy-like way.

Deep breath. Everyone looks at me, wondering what I'm going to do. Wondering whether I'm going to have another row with Jenny. I'm wondering the same thing.

Then I decide I don't want to give them the satisfaction. I walk over. 'Hi, Elizabeth,' I say.

'Hi,' she says.

Then I add, 'Hi, guys,' for good measure.

Jenny can't even look at me. She can't look at anyone, and I notice that she is about as far away from Charlie Notts as two people waiting for the same bus can be. They must have broken up already. Is it OK that I'm really happy about that?

There's a moment of silence in the group and no one knows who's going to speak first.

'So, Gwynnie . . . what did you get up to this weekend?' asks Elizabeth.

I smile at her to thank her for breaking the ice. 'Not much,' I say.

More silence. This is awkward. I guess I have to say something else. 'I watched the replay of the Spurs match on Sunday. 3–2. I could not believe it until I saw it for myself.'

The girls look at me, not really knowing how to reply. I don't think anyone talks to them about football and I've caught them off guard.

'Tottenham are the winners of the FA Cup and it's the best thing in the world.'

I'm a bit gutted that I missed out watching it at Wembley, but in a weird way it was worth it to find out the truth about everything. I don't tell them that part though.

'I've still got it recorded if any of you want to watch it.'

Kimba screws up her face like I've just invited her to watch a spitting tournament in the rain. 'Why would we want to watch *football*? And if we did, we wouldn't watch it at your house. I'm not sure if my stomach can handle Tesco-brand cola.' She's smirking.

I am just about to wipe the grin off her face when someone else steps in and does it for me.

'Shut up, Kimba!' It's Jenny. I'm shocked. 'Can't you give that bitch thing a rest for once?'

Kimba goes quiet. We all do.

I do a half-grin at Jenny for sticking up for me.

'Sorry, Gwynnie,' Kimba says.

'That's OK,' I reply. 'What's that thing it says in the Bible about forgiving people for stuff?' I'm saying this to Kimba but Jenny knows I'm talking about her.

'It says you should do it,' Jenny says. We smile at each other. Then she says, 'You know, I wouldn't mind seeing the match, Gwynnie.'

'OK.' I'll forgive her one day, but I'm not quite ready to set a date yet. 'Elizabeth,' I say, 'I'm going to chat to Paul and Ranj over there – want to come?'

Elizabeth follows me over to where Paul and Ranj are standing. I flinch for a second when I realize we have to pass Charlie Notts to get there. Still, I guess I have to see him some time. No turning back now.

He looks at me and dares to smile in a really sheepish kind of way. He has no one to talk to now the name Charlie Notts is written in Paul's and my bad books. He's lost his best friends.

'Hi, Gwynnie,' he says.

I do the eyebrow-raising thing, leave it at that and walk past him.

No, I won't leave it at that.

I turn back. 'Hi, Charlie,' I say.

'Hi?' he says it like a question. Like he's forgotten what *hi* means and he has to check.

'What are you going to do now the football season is over?' I ask.

He breaks into a relieved grin. 'Only seventy-six days, seven hours and,' he looks at his watch, 'thirteen minutes until the next kick-off.'

I can't think of anything else to say so I just smile and walk away. I'm pretty relieved when I get to where my mates are.

'You all right, Paul? Ranj?'

'Yeah,' they say. Ranj beams at Elizabeth while Paul looks a bit down in the dumps. We all know he's sad so we don't say anything for a second.

'Did you see the match, Gwynnie?' Ranjit asks.

'Oh my God, it was so cool! I was on the edge of my seat until Crouch scored his second goal . . . And what a goal! He was only about a metre this side of the halfway line. The man is a legend.'

'Hey,' Paul says, 'the Year 8s said they reckon they could take us in a match. We're gonna play at break time. You wanna watch?'

'Watch?' I ask, like he's just suggested I wear an Arsenal top. 'You need me on the wing. I'm playing!'

Paul smiles.

Ranj goes all red before he says, 'Would you like to watch, Elizabeth?'

Elizabeth bites her bottom lip and nods. 'OK.'

'I warn you though,' Ranj says, 'I'm not that brilliant at football.'

'You can say that again!' says Paul in a jokey way.

Ranj starts going for Paul's shoelaces, trying to step on them so Paul falls over. I join in, and laugh when Paul falls on his bum.

And I can see now that everything will be exactly like old times, but also totally different. I'll be wearing my old football boots with a hole, but I will be colour-coordinating them with flawless make-up and a stunning wardrobe. New

Gwynnie and Old Gwynnie have shaken hands and called a truce. And it feels pretty good. A little bit.

THE END

Boys for Beginners

Lil Chase

Quercus

First published in Great Britain in 2011 by Quercus

21 Bloomsbury Square
London
WC1A 2NS

A CIP catalogue reference for this book is available
from the British Library

ISBN 978-0 85738 482 9

10 9 8 7 6 5 4 3 2 1

Typeset by Nigel Hazle
Printed and bound in Great Britain by Clays Ltd, St Ives plc.